Silent Girl

Silent Girl

stories by

Tricia Dower

inanna poetry & fiction series

INANNA Publications and Education Inc.
Toronto, Canada

Kesh Kumay first appeared in *Cicada Magazine*.

 Canada Council   Conseil des Arts
for the Arts   du Canada

The publisher gratefully acknowledges the support of the Canada Council for the Arts for its publishing program.

The publisher is also grateful for the kind support received from an Anonymous Fund at The Calgary Foundation.

THE CALGARY
FOUNDATION

Library and Archives Canada Cataloguing in Publication

Dower, Tricia, 1942-
   Silent Girl : stories / by Tricia Dower

(Inanna poetry and fiction series)
ISBN 978-0-9808822-0-9

   I. Title. II. Series.

PS3604.O939S45 2008   813'.6   C2008-901857-5

Cover design by Val Fullard
Interior design by Luciana Ricciutelli
Printed and bound in Canada

Inanna Publications and Education Inc.
210 Founders College, York University
4700 Keele Street
Toronto, Ontario, Canada M3J 1P3
Telephone: (416) 736-5356 Fax (416) 736-5765
Email: inanna@yorku.ca
Website: www.yorku.ca/inanna

To Colin,
come rain or come shine.

Contents

ೞ೫ಔ

The stories in this book are inspired by the plays of William Shakespeare.

Not Meant to Know

I have done nothing but in care of thee / Of thee, my dear one, my daughter.
—Prospero to Miranda in *The Tempest*

ೞ

I WAS UNDER STRICT ORDERS TO STAY AWAY FROM THE RIVER THAT meandered through our town. But on that sticky hot day when Tereza Dobra said, "Let's go smoke punks, it'll be cooler there," I said okay. She had moved in across the street two weeks earlier and was my new best friend. She seemed to do whatever she pleased. Possessed a magic power I lacked. Maybe because she was twelve going on thirteen and I was only eleven.

What Tereza called punks – cattail flowers that look like cigars – grew in stagnant water at a particular edge of the river. To get there we had to go down a narrow road past Crazy Haggerty's house – the biggest in our neighborhood. It sat high above the water, all by its lonesome. The drapes were drawn tight, not a window open to catch a breeze. You couldn't tell if Haggerty was in there watching. I'd only ever seen him on my way home from school – heading toward town, weaving back and forth, always wearing the same red shoes and satiny black suit with sequins. He'd scowl if you gawked, tell you to get lost. A house as grand as his would have to give out more than a handful of candy corn on Hallowe'en, but I was too afraid to get close to it.

"Not me," Tereza said. "If I'd 'a moved here sooner, we'd 'a trick-or-treated it by now." I could see her climbing the stairs in that quick, sneaky way of hers, standing on the shadowy veranda demanding a treat.

We crab-walked down the riverbank, taking care not to slip in the mud. Any noise or sudden motion made me jump: the call of a tree frog, a fluttering swallowtail, a red-winged blackbird flushed from reeds. If I was found out, I'd be banished to my room without dinner.

Tereza pulled a penknife from her pocket and cut us a couple of punks, leaving short stems. She had a small box of wooden matches, too. The punks weren't dry enough to flame up and she wasted a couple of matches before they caught and smoldered. "Mmm," she said, waving hers under her nose, "I'd walk a mile for a Camel."

I stuck the stem of mine in my mouth and *puh-puh-puhed* as I'd seen my dad do when he was getting his pipe going. The stem tasted like potato peel.

Tereza snorted. "Ain't nothing to inhale, genius. This your first punk?"

"Course not," I said. "It's just more fun this way."

She tried puh-puh-puhing, too, and then sucked on the stem so hard her eyes crossed, making me hoot out loud. "No it ain't," she said.

Both of us wore pedal-pushers but they looked better on Tereza. She wasn't pudgy and her skin was the color of a root-beer float. "There's more than a little gypsy in that girl," I'd overheard Mom tell Dad. "And her hair! A regular rat's nest."

I definitely had it over Tereza in that department. My mother washed and set my hair in pin curls every Saturday night. I was fortunate to be an ash blonde, she said, as the gray would blend in and be hardly noticeable when I got old.

"Your name means pretty in Spanish," Tereza said, plopping down on the ground.

"No kidding?" I stayed upright, couldn't show up at home with mud on my behind. I hid myself behind a tall bush and held my punk down by my knees so the smoke wouldn't give me away. I could still see the street, Crazy Haggerty's, and anyone coming.

"My real father speaks three languages," Tereza said. Her history was more complicated than mine.

"Did he tell you Linda means pretty?"

"No, I've never met him."

A police car came slowly and silently down the street. "Quiet," I whispered, scooting over to Tereza. We snuffed out our punks and crawled like spiders, on fingertips and feet, to get closer to the road.

Two uniformed cops got out of the car and went up Crazy Haggerty's stairs. You could hear barking even before they got to the door. They knocked a few times and the door opened a sliver. The barking turned to growling and one of the cops took his gun out of the holster. After a while the growling stopped and whoever had opened the door let them in.

"Somebody must 'a got bumped off," Tereza said.

"No one gets murdered in this boring town," I said. The river never flooded, either; at least it hadn't as long as I'd been alive. That I was forbidden to be there didn't make sense. It wasn't as if we were still at war with the Japanese and had to worry about them skulking up the river, signaling each other with jars of lightning bugs. (According to my mother, not long after she and Dad married, just after Pearl Harbor, she'd lie awake at night picturing that very thing.)

A truck came down the street and pulled in back of the cop car. Two men emerged, opened the back of the truck and pulled out a huge butterfly net and a big cage. They went inside the house and reappeared a while later with a muzzled German shepherd. It took both of them to carry the cage.

Tereza and I crouched for ages – my knees and thighs were burning – before one of the cops walked out the front door carrying a small, tan suitcase. The other cop followed, holding the elbow of a girl who looked to be fifteen or sixteen. On her hip, a child of maybe two.

"Who's that?" Tereza said.

"Somebody visiting the old man, I guess."

"What's wrong with the kid?"

"Beats me."

The child's head was freak-show small. The girl had cocker

spaniel hair down to her waist. I couldn't see enough of her face to tell if she was pretty. She wore an old-fashioned navy blue dress with a Peter Pan collar and shoulder pads. The child's arms around the girl's neck and the sway of her hips as she walked to the cop car filled me with wonder.

Tereza stood. "I'm gonna find out what's going on."

"No!" I yanked the back of her pants and pulled her back down. "They might tell on us. I'll get in trouble."

"With the cops?"

"No. My folks."

"What's the worst they can do to you?"

I couldn't think of anything that would impress Tereza. Her legs always had a raw welt or two. Due to her getting "too lippy," she said when I asked her, like you might explain away a rash from eating too many tomatoes.

"You can't imagine," I said.

She wrinkled her nose as though I'd just farted and dropped back to the ground. "My brother's a big chicken, too," she said.

The car and the truck drove away. We stayed a while without talking. Tereza relit her punk but not mine. The sun slipping down the side of the sky chased us home.

Dad returned from work that night long after Mom had exchanged housedress for shirtwaist, pumps, and nylons. Dinner was more than ready. As he hung up his suit jacket in the hall closet, he said, "James Haggerty died yesterday. Heart attack or stroke, they're not sure. I stopped in at Tony's for a new wiper on the way home and he told me."

He came into the dining room where I'd gone to stand behind my chair as soon as I heard him at the door. I never thought of Crazy Haggerty having a first name.

"I didn't think he was that old," Mom said, carrying dishes out from the kitchen.

"Forty-eight, according to Tony." Dad took his position behind her chair. His white shirt was damp under the arms and wrinkled along the back.

"Must've been the drink, then," Mom said.

"Did he die in his house?" I asked.

He gave me a surprised look. "Hello, Sunbeam. I forgot to give you a hug." He opened his arms and I walked into their damp, solid warmth. He smelled of starch and underarms.

"Did he die in that big house?" I said into his chest.

"No, on the train back from Penn Station. He'd gone into the city for some reason. Had bags of strange stuff in his pockets, so they say."

"What kind of strange stuff?"

"I think that's everything," Mom said, surveying the table. Dad pulled out her chair and she sat. He took his place opposite her and I sat. We bowed our heads.

"For what we are about to receive," Dad said, "we are truly grateful." We removed our napkins from under our forks and spread them on our laps.

"What kind of strange stuff?" I asked again.

Mom put a thin slice of roasted chicken, a small mound of mashed potatoes, and a fistful of green beans on my plate. A canned peach-half waiting in a small dish on the sideboard would be my dessert. Since I had inherited my father's build, she said, I'd have to watch what I ate for the rest of my life.

"He had a child, apparently," Dad said, unbuttoning his cuffs and rolling up his sleeves. The hair on his arms was sweaty dark. "Possibly two. Tony had quite a bit to say about that."

"Really." A statement, not a question. The look she gave him warned not to say more in my presence. When I was younger, they spoke in Pig Latin. *Eally-Ray*.

"What did you do today, Linda?" Dad asked.

"Hung around with Tereza."

"Interesting expression, that. Can you be more specific?"

"I don't know. We just talked and stuff. How old's his child? Boy or girl?"

"That's not open for discussion," Mom said.

"Why not?"

"Don't argue with your mother. Did you help around the house?"

"She peeled potatoes and set the table," Mom said.

"Good. He had a teenaged daughter and there's a little boy who might be hers."

"Roger!"

After dinner they sat in the backyard while I did the dishes – a chore I rarely objected to. It let me pick at the leftovers. That night it also let me eavesdrop through the window over the sink as I dipped plates in and out of the hot, soapy water, quiet as I could, my ears on full alert. At first their voices were as faint as fly hums. The sound drifted in on the fruity smell of my dad's pipe smoke. Then came buzzing, and a hornet-like crossness loud enough for me to pick out words.

"He should have been shot."

"No point poking a stick in his dead eye, Betty."

"Why are you defending him?"

"I'm not. I don't know enough about it to blame or defend. Neither do you."

"A teenager with a baby and nobody knew she existed. Isn't that enough?"

Their voices dropped again and then tapered off. Mom came in and went up to bed. It was what she usually did when she was peeved. Dad stayed outside for a while, smoking his pipe. Later, he and I watched TV together, ignoring my mother's empty armchair. I sat on his lap like I did most nights. His lap never objected to my build. I fell asleep to him stroking my hair.

Tereza and I met the next morning, as usual, in the small woods we called The Island. I wore new Keds with laces that criss-crossed my ankles like a Roman soldier's, hoping they'd win back a few of the points I'd lost with her the day before. I waited for her on the hollowed out log in which we stashed scavenged props for *Swiss Family Robinson*: a bent spoon, some string, the silver foil from gum wrappers. The ebb and flow of cars and trucks on the highway half a block from my house was the sound of the sea that had shipwrecked us.

Tereza saw uses for things I considered trash – like cigarette butts.

She stripped them and collected the loose tobacco in a Wonder Bread bag. Said we could sell it for food when we escaped from The Island. She showed up that morning with a handful of cattails, punks and all.

"What are those for?"

"If we let the punks dry out they'll be better smokes. When they turn to fluff we can make pillows. We can weave the leaves into sleeping mats."

"The rule is we live on whatever we find on The Island. Punks don't grow here. Berries and acorns do."

"It's our game, right? We make the rules."

"It's my game. I played it a whole year before you came."

"Yeah, and what have you got to show for it? You didn't make a tree house. You didn't make nothin' we could sell when we get off The Island."

"What if I don't want to get off?" I said. "What if I want to live here forever?"

"That's just plain dumb. Nothin' to do here. Nobody to see. Might as well be Crazy Haggerty's kid, locked up in that house."

"Maybe she liked it there."

"My old man said her father must 'a parked his car in her garage."

"What's that supposed to mean?"

She made a gesture with her hand that I could tell was dirty. "My old man tries that with me, I'll kick him in the balls," she said.

I sucked in my breath. You weren't supposed to say balls; at least I wasn't. My cousin's dog was always licking his, making my uncle laugh. I didn't like to think of my father having them.

"Maybe your old man is wrong," I said. The way the girl walked out of that house had stuck in my head. She didn't look scared or in any hurry to leave.

"Nope," Tereza said. She stuffed the cattails inside the log and sat beside me.

"Do you think Haggerty's daughter ever went to school?" I said.

"Probly not. Lucky her."

I didn't think that was lucky. I liked almost everything about school: getting escorted across the highway by the safety patrol, waiting on the playground for the bell to ring, learning about the solar system, using the pencil sharpener. Most kids hated grammar but I appreciated knowing there was a right way to speak and you could learn it.

I often tried out new expressions on my parents, to see how much information they'd let loose without realizing it. That night at dinner I said, "What kind of car did Mr. Haggerty park in his daughter's garage?"

Dad started to laugh – he had a deep chuckle that tickled your insides – then stopped and put on a serious face. "As far as I know, he didn't have a car."

I told them what Tereza had said.

Mom looked at her plate. Dad looked at the ceiling. "You and your mother need to have a chat," he said.

I knew we wouldn't. Earlier that year the school nurse had sent us sixth grade girls home with a kit and instructions to "chat" with our mothers. The kit contained a sanitary napkin, a belt, and a booklet called *Growing Up and Liking It*. The booklet had tiny illustrations of hidden female body parts, none of which I could envision inside me. My mother put the kit in the bottom drawer of her bureau. "We won't need this for at least another year," she said.

I was invited to Tereza's house for dinner later that week. Supper, she called it.

"I'm not wild about the idea," Mom said. "We don't know anything about them."

"It's only across the street," Dad said.

"That's not what I mean."

"Why don't you walk over there, then? Welcome them to the neighborhood. Poke around in their garbage can."

"Very funny," Mom said.

"I like Tereza," Dad said. "She has spunk."

I ended up going, taking along a plate of oatmeal cookies to show I had manners. I had waited for Tereza on her porch a bunch of times but never gone inside. She lived on the lower floor of a multiple-family house. The hallway leading to her front door was dark and smelled like my grandmother's attic. It gave me the heebie-jeebies.

I knocked a couple of times before Tereza's half-brother Allen opened the door and shouted, "Tereeeeeeeeze!" I'd seen him riding his bike but not close up. His sharp little nose and wingy ears made me think of Tereza's chicken remark. The door opened into the living room, bare of furniture except for a TV. Allen left me standing at the door and sat on the floor next to a man in work pants and undershirt. Tereza's step-father, I assumed. They were watching *Flash Gordon*, sitting so close they would ruin their eyesight, for sure. Tereza rescued me, finally, and led me into the kitchen where her mother stood barefoot by the stove.

"Hey," she said as if she'd known me forever. Her voice was low and thick. "Whacha got there?"

I held out the cookies.

"You make them?"

"No, my mom."

She smirked at that. Her lips were fat like Tereza's and her hair just as black but her skin was lighter. She looked all loose, like a pile of laundry ready for the wash. Nipples showed through her white scoop-necked blouse, the outline of her legs through her wrap-around skirt.

"Get the chair from your room for Linda, Tez," she said. Tereza left the room.

"How long you lived on this street?" Mrs. Dobra asked me.

"Since I was born."

"Ah, good for you."

She said that so sadly I looked around for something nice to say. "I wish we had painted walls. Our kitchen has so many tea kettles on the wall you get dizzy staring at them. My dad couldn't match up all of the strips, so some of the kettles are cut in half."

She coughed out a laugh. "If we weren't renters, I'd give your daddy all the beer he could drink to come over and slap up some wallpaper."

I didn't tell her my father disapproved of beer, didn't want her to think we were stuck-up.

Tereza returned with a chair.

"Allen! Jimmy!" Mrs. Dobra shouted, making me jump. "Chow's on!"

We ate in the kitchen on a yellow painted wooden table that wasn't quite big enough for five people so we had to squeeze together. Jimmy – it was hard to think of him as Mr. Dobra – straddled the chair between Allen and me, his thigh pressing against mine. It was his nose and ears Allen had gotten, along with hair the color of peanut butter. Jimmy was thinner than my father and the muscles on his arms stood out. It didn't look as though he shaved often. He was a construction worker, Tereza had told me. They moved whenever he ran out of work.

Mrs. Dobra took two pans right off the stove and set them on the bare table top without the slightest concern about scorch marks. "Help yourself," she said, looking at me. Canned corn and stewed tomatoes. Pieces of hot dogs swimming in baked beans. A huge bowl of potato chips. Allen stuck his hand in the chips. Jimmy filled his plate with the bean mixture. No one said grace.

"You got a name?" Jimmy asked me.

"It's Linda," Mrs. Dobra said. "Tez's friend. You know that."

"Did I ask you?"

He raised his eyebrows at me. He was smiling but his eyes were mean.

"Linda," I said.

"You ever eat wild boar, Linda?"

"No, sir."

"It's pig, like these hot dogs are pig, but it tastes like polar bear."

Tereza made a rude noise. "How would you know?" she said.

"Looking for trouble?" Jimmy said to her.

Mrs. Dobra's voice rushed in. "Before Jimmy and me met, he worked in the North."

"I can tell my own stories," Jimmy said. He waggled his fork at Tereza. "It was in Thunder Bay, Miss Smartass. That's in Canada, in case you haven't learnt that yet. I'm not the dumb fuck you think I am."

"Jimmy," Mrs. Dobra said softly.

Nobody spoke after that. We just applied ourselves to getting supper over and done with. The tattooed anchor on Jimmy's right arm twitched as he ate. I offered to do dishes, but Tereza's mother said she wanted to sit in the kitchen by herself for a while and smoke a cigarette.

Tereza took me into the room she shared with Allen. A blanket draped over a rope divided the space. There wasn't much on her side besides a narrow, unmade bed, a chest of drawers with a Dale Evans lamp on it, and a poster for a movie called *Rogues of Sherwood Forest*. It featured a man in tights pointing a sword.

"John Derek," Tereza said. "Ma says my real father looks like him."

"Your real father's Robin Hood?"

"No, you nincompoop. Robin Hood ain't real."

"I know. I was making a joke." John Derek's moustache was thin but food could still get stuck in it and smell if you were an actress and had to kiss him.

"Look at this," Tereza said. She opened a drawer in the chest. "Ma found it." She pulled out a newspaper and began to read aloud as slowly as a third grader. It made my jaw ache.

"Here, let me," I said, holding out my hand.

> *James Michael Haggerty, born March 3, 1907, died June 19, 1955, of natural causes. Predeceased in 1943 by his wife Eileen. Survived by his daughter Miranda. Funeral closed to the public. Burial to be handled by Markinson Funeral Home.*

Miranda. She had a name. "What about the boy?" I said.

"They don't want nobody knowing that crazy old man knocked her up." Tereza took the newspaper from me and put it back in her drawer. "My mom got knocked up with me."

"Who says?"

"She told me."

"Did it hurt?"

Tereza laughed so hard I wanted to punch her. "I'm leaving," I said.

"No, wait. Let's go peek in the windows. The dog ain't there no more."

I didn't want her to call me a chicken again, and I was itching to learn more about Miranda. "As long as you don't tell your folks where we're going. My dad might come looking for me. I gotta be home before dark, okay?"

The sky was still holding its light as we crept along the river-bank, approaching Crazy Haggerty's from the back. Anyone on the other side of the river would have been too far away to see us. A metal stake in the ground and a heavy long chain made me hesitate until I remembered the German shepherd was gone. We had to step around mounds of dog poop. "I never saw him walk that dog," I said.

A small stack of firewood leaned against the wall by a back door. Tereza tried to open the door but it was locked. Shutters secured with combination locks completely covered picture windows on the outside.

"I can break 'em open, easy," she said.

"If you do, I'm not staying," I said. "I won't tell, but I won't stay."

"Look up there," Tereza said. She pointed to the second floor, to a small window that wasn't shuttered. It was close to the corner of the house. She monkeyed up a drainpipe, grabbed hold of the window ledge, and chinned herself over and over until she'd had a good look. Back on the ground, she said, "The kitchen. Nothing to see in there except a wood stove. Everything clean as spit. Nothing in the sink. No table or chairs, neither."

"They must have eaten in the dining room," I said.

"Or not at all," she said. "They could be zombies from outer space."

Tereza exasperated me with her lack of knowledge of how some things worked. "Zombies are already dead," I said. "Crazy Haggerty wouldn't have had a heart attack if he was a zombie." I noticed two small basement windows that were barred but not shuttered. "Maybe we can see something through the bars," I said.

Each of us took a different window. Kneeling on a piece of wood so I wouldn't get my knees dirty, I peered in. The light was dim but I could make out two white pillars with black drapes hanging between them. In front of the drapes was a table with tall white candles and a book as big as my father's unabridged *Webster's*.

"I see a cape on a hook," Tereza called over to me.

I scooted over to see it. I knew all about Dracula and the cape made me frightened for the girl – for Miranda – though I supposed she was safe now.

"Too bad I didn't move here sooner. I would 'a sprung her," Tereza said.

"How?"

She didn't have an answer.

"Maybe she'll be back," I said. "It's still her house, right?"

I considered the possibility she might be a lunatic Haggerty had saved from the horrors of an asylum. I had learned about asylums from a comic book somebody passed around the playground. They tied you up and turned hoses on you, attached wires to your head and cooked your brain. I wanted to believe he had been protecting her from that or something worse.

That night a huge black bug climbed onto my back. It was so big and heavy, I couldn't breathe. I must have screamed because my mother came into my room. I was glad it was her. "Hush, angel, it's only a dream," she said, rubbing my back.

One August morning, Dad informed me Mom was going to the hospital for an operation. "A female thing," he whispered in the kitchen. That was the first I'd heard about it.

"Take care of your father," she said as he helped her into the car.

She was supposed to be home after ten days but the doctor decided to keep her in longer due to complications. "I can't afford any more time away from work," Dad said as if it was something he had to write a check for. "You'll have to take care of things around the house."

I rummaged around in my brain for everything I knew about being a wife. Keep your hands out of the wringer washer. Start with the collar of the shirt when you iron, then the yoke, then the sleeves. Skim the cream off the top of the milk for his coffee. Be sure all evidence of your housework is out of sight by the time he comes home.

I figured out how to make scrambled eggs and Jell-O. I knew how to use the can opener, so I made soup. Dad's favorite was split pea. I sat outside with him every night after dinner while he smoked his pipe and talked about his secretary and his boss. He helped me with the dishes before our nightly hospital visit. During the day, when he wasn't around, I opened cans of expensive Queen Anne cherries Mom had hidden in the pantry behind a broken toaster. I ate them all by myself.

I sat at her mahogany dressing table and smeared my face with Pond's – as cool and creamy as Junket pudding. I opened her little red box of mascara, stuck two fingers in my mouth like I'd seen her do and moistened the tiny brush before dipping it into the box. I thought about Miranda in that big house with Crazy Haggerty. Did she know she was supposed to brush her hair a hundred strokes each day? I washed my own hair for the first time and needed every bobby pin in the house to set it.

One night in the car on the way to visit Mom, I asked Dad, "How come nobody knew Mr. Haggerty had a daughter?" I was in the front where Mom usually sat. Got to look at the little scar on the side of his face and watch him shift gears.

"People were scared of him. Your mother went over there once to collect for the Red Cross and he greeted her on the porch with a shotgun."

"But why wouldn't he send her to school?"

"No idea." He reached over and patted my leg. "If only we'd

14

known. Everybody just thought he was eccentric. We left him alone."

"Where did he work?"

"He didn't, as far as anybody knew. His mother left him that house before we moved in. She must have left him some money, too."

"I used to call him Crazy Haggerty," I said.

"You weren't the only one."

"Dad?"

"Yeah?"

"You said he had strange stuff in his pockets when he died on the train."

"Did I? Why are you so interested in Mr. Haggerty?"

"I want to know, that's all."

"Well, kiddo, there are some things we're just not meant to know."

After fifteen days, my mother was able to dangle her legs over the side of the hospital bed. I didn't have as much time with Tereza as before, since she didn't want to help me dust or vacuum or wash floors.

"I'm never getting married," she said. "If I have to clean somebody's house I want to get paid for it." She started hanging around with the greasy-haired boys who prowled the neighborhood in a pack. Some of them were in high school already. I didn't like the way they took up the entire sidewalk and laughed when you tried to walk past. She followed them to town during the day and to the river at dusk. On weekends, Dad took over the chores so I could be with her but she had lost interest in *Swiss Family Robinson*. She turned up on The Island one day wearing dungarees that didn't fit.

"Somebody gave 'em to Allen, but they ain't his size," she said.

"They're too big in the waist for you," I said.

"Yeah, and they cut into my crotch. I feel sorry for boys. Ever seen a penis?"

"I don't think so."

"Some are stubby like punks. Others are kinda worm-like."

"How many have you seen?"

"Well, my brother's, natch, but that don't count." Then she named the neighborhood boys. "They smoke cigs," she said. "They let me take drags if I kiss 'em."

"Their penises?"

"No! Their mouths."

"Can you taste what they've been eating?"

"Natch."

"How nauseating." Nauseating was my favorite new word that summer and I was not allowed to say it at the dinner table. "Don't your folks mind you going with them?"

"They don't ask and I don't tell."

The next Monday, after Dad had gone to work, I looked up penis in *Webster's Unabridged*; then, the words in the definition I didn't understand. Eventually I got to "intercourse" and "impregnate" and began to think about Miranda and Crazy Haggerty. It made my stomach hurt. I did the laundry and pictured Dad's boxer shorts hiding something worm-like. I stopped sitting on his lap. Over the next week or so, I paged through every book in our house – books I had no interest in before – searching for the rules of intercourse. Seeking reassurance that what happened to Miranda was out of the ordinary, something I didn't have to be afraid of. I retrieved the *Growing Up and Liking It* kit from the bottom of my mother's bureau. The books and the kit were silent on the subject. Maybe Miranda's father had kept her in because he knew she'd be like Tereza, wandering off whenever she wanted, kissing boys and looking at their penises.

Tereza was old enough for eighth grade but she got put into seventh with me. We walked together every morning, me with my head down looking for lucky pennies, she with her head twisting like a periscope, searching for boys. A month after school began, she turned thirteen and started hanging around the playground with older kids after school. Told me not to wait for her. The first time she said that I went right to The Island and cleaned everything out of the log, spread it all through the woods. I wanted the wind to take her precious tobacco, but the Wonder Bread bag was gone.

My mother had returned from the hospital in time for Labor Day but, within a few weeks, she slipped into a sort of sadness the doctor couldn't explain. She'd be in bed when I left for school and in bed when I returned. I brought her ginger ale and dry toast every afternoon but it didn't make her better. "Is your father home yet?" was all she would say. Her uterus had been removed, he told me, finally, and he thought she'd be happy to be rid of it, but she wasn't. I went back to keeping house. Dad and I went back to the routine we'd fallen into when Mom was in the hospital although it felt different with her in the house. Like she was the daughter.

"She says she feels too heavy to move," Dad would say. Or, "She says she can't see colors anymore." He'd squint at me as if I could do something about it, as if I could make everything hunky-dory in the few hours I had after school before he got home.

One afternoon I found a playing card in one of his jacket pockets where I'd gone looking for Life Savers. On it was a picture of a woman naked except for a garter belt, nylons, and high heels. I wondered if my father thought she had "spunk." I decided I'd never grow an ugly clump of dark hair between my legs, never grow anything men might want to stare at. I wanted to rip the card into a zillion pieces but I put it back inside the pocket. I began to look at my father differently after that, was ashamed of all the times he had seen me naked when I was little. I got to hate the way he cleared his throat every morning and held his pipe at the side of his mouth like he thought he was a big movie star. I withdrew to my room when I got tired of him.

I could see the highway from my bedroom window and liked to watch the cars go by. I'd pretend I was in one of those cars going all the way down to Florida, stopping at every White Castle along the way. I could see Tony's garage, too. It was on the corner of our street and the highway. The lot was always full of cars. Drivers passed by the garage on their way to bigger towns each day and a sign saying *Repairs While U Work* attracted business. Every morning you could see men dropping their cars off and waiting in their suits and hats for the bus. Late one afternoon, I thought I saw Tereza getting into the back seat of a car parked around the side of the garage. I couldn't be sure it was her but whoever it was had Tereza's shape and wild hair.

After dinner that day, Dad took his newspaper upstairs to spend the evening with Mom. I went over to Tereza's and knocked on her door. Allen said she wasn't there. I went back to my house, sat on the front stoop and waited for her. The moon was out by the time she came scurrying along on the opposite side of the street, wearing tight, little white shorts and a bubblegum-pink sweater. It was almost Hallowe'en, too cold for shorts.

"Hey!" I called out.

She looked in my direction but didn't slow down.

"Hey!" I got up and ran after her. "Wait up!"

"Beat it!" she said, throwing the words over her shoulder. She was nearly at the foot of her porch steps.

"What were you doing at Tony's?"

She stopped then and turned around. I thought the skin around her eyes was bruised until I realized she was wearing mascara that had run. "You seen me?"

"Yeah, getting into a car."

"You rat on me, I swear I'll kill you."

"Rat on you about what?"

Just then Jimmy burst onto the porch, a leather strap wound around his hand. "Get up here, you little whore," he said. "I know what you been doing."

As Jimmy came down the stairs, Tereza started to back up. She shoved me out of the way just as Jimmy let loose with the belt, flicking it like a whip. "Go ahead, you piece of shit," Tereza said, dancing around to miss the whip. "The worst you can do is kill me, and then I won't care, will I?"

I ran to my house, screaming for my father over and over. He was at the door by the time I got there, hand on chest.

"What, what?" he said, out of breath.

I pointed to Jimmy chasing Tereza around in circles in the street

18

in front of our house, lashing the pavement with the belt. She was zigzagging and dodging, taunting him all the while.

"You have to stop him," I said. Dad stiffened and frowned but didn't move.

"Hurry!" I said, tugging at his arm.

He pulled me to him and said, "Not our business."

I broke away and ran out into the street, waving my arms at Jimmy, yelling at him to stop. He looked at me long enough for Tereza to scurry away quicker than a mouse. Jimmy pulled back the belt as though to whip me but Dad was right there. He stepped between us and put a hand on Jimmy's chest. "That'll be enough of that," he said.

Jimmy's cheeks were splotchy with anger and he straightened to his full height. Getting ready to sock Dad, I was sure. But then he seemed to lose air. He slapped Dad's hand down and walked away.

"That was a foolish thing you did," Dad said as he opened our front door. "You could have gotten hurt."

"I hate you," I said and ran up to my bedroom and locked the door.

The next morning when I got downstairs Mom was in the kitchen, making pancakes. She was pale and shaky and gave me a smile I didn't know how to take. "We're having tuna casserole and rice pudding tonight," she said. "What do you think about that?"

Before and after school every day for weeks, I looked for Tereza on The Island and down by the river, not caring if I got in trouble for going there. I felt desperate to find her, frantic to know if she'd gotten in my dad's car. The police and the whole neighborhood looked for her, too, but she was gone.

I couldn't stop thinking about Miranda, either, wondering if she and Tereza were hiding out together somewhere. One Saturday when I was supposed to be at the library, I walked to the police station and told the officer at the front desk I was doing a school report on unsolved crimes and I wanted to know what had happened to Miranda. He smiled and told me to wait. A man in a sports jacket came out, eventually, and told me she'd gone to a foster home. The boy, too.

"There was no crime," he said. "Nothing to solve."

The Dobras moved away after Christmas. Mom didn't get better for good until spring. My grandmother came out from Nebraska and took care of us for a while.

The next summer I got my own penknife and matches and smoked punks down by the river. Sometimes the boys Tereza used to hang around with were there. They told me she'd been getting into cars at Tony's for weeks before Jimmy got wise to it. She'd hide in the back seat of a car Tony had finished working on and wait for the owner to pick it up. When he'd driven a few blocks she'd sit up and scare the bejesus out of him. She'd tell him her mom was sick and needed money for medicine. She'd offer to sell them the tobacco in the Wonder Bread bag but it was something else they bought.

They told me what they knew about Crazy Haggerty, too. That he worshipped the devil and hid Miranda so the authorities wouldn't take her away from him. The boy was half beast, they said, and Crazy Haggerty had snake fangs, rat tails, and porcupine quills in his pockets when he died. I didn't believe half of what they said, but I liked to hear them talk. They showed me that if you light a punk when the stalk is still a little young and smoke it down to the end, the heat sends sap fizzing up into your mouth. It tastes like there's nothing in the world you're not meant to know.

Silent Girl

This world to me is like a lasting storm.
                                                    —Marina in *Pericles*

ᘓᘔ

A DAGGER OF LIGHT PIERCED THE ROOM AS THE DOOR FELL OPEN and Maw-Maw entered, pushing a wobbly cart. Her flip-flops spanked the wood floor. Her arm pulled a cord that ignited a bulb that swung from the ceiling. Searching for secrets, Matsi was sure.

"*Le souper,*" Maw-Maw said, dipping her legs in mock curtsy.

Six girls squinted at the stark light then slowly arched their kitten-boned backs. They crawled to the edge of their cots. Maw-Maw shuffled by each, placing scarred bowls in their cupped hands.

"De wind change, you face be stuck in dose pout," she said, spooning rice and red beans from a pot. Flesh as spongy as dumpling dough spilled from the sleeveless arms of her dress, trembling with each plop of the spoon. "What it cost you to make a smile, to tank me?" she asked, though the girls had never said a word to her. "Back ohm, you be starvin, probly dead."

Matsi's voice nearly flew out from its hiding place. The brown girls might be poor but she was not. Their parents might have sold them but hers had not. Back home she'd sleep after supper, not before, wouldn't stay up all night like a raccoon or an owl. She ate quickly. Maw-Maw would collect the first bowl as soon as she filled the last. Empty bowls on the cart, Maw-Maw clapped and held out her hands. The girls removed their underpants for inspection. One of the brown girls had stained hers. "Watch de slap," Maw-Maw said before her hand connected with the girl's face. Thwack! The stupid girl slumped to the floor bawling.

Matsi was too clever to stain her pants. She took them off each morning after Maw-Maw locked the girls into the sleeping room and put them on again when she heard the key click. She rarely let sleep swallow her whole, always made it to the bucket in the dark. Cots were inspected next; all were dry. Bedwetting earned worse than a slap.

Maw-Maw herded them into a high-ceilinged room, empty but for the echo and the dragon-clawed tub in which the girls stood in turns. The bigger girls always went first. By the time Matsi got in, the water would be cool and scummy. She watched Maw-Maw run a cloth roughly over one girl until the skin looked burned underneath.

"Anh! Look at dat." Maw-Maw dropped the cloth, thrust a hand between the girl's legs and pulled out a hair. The girl whimpered.

"Filthy twat. My boys doan wanna see dis. You be poodoo soon." Anything Maw-Maw didn't like was poodoo.

Matsi remembered other places where the girls were hustled together into vans on unsuspecting nights and driven each to a different place. At Maw-Maw's, girls went missing one at a time after hard little lumps formed behind their nipples, or their hips got round, or they grew hair in dirty places. Like magic, new girls took their places. Matsi had been there longer than the others. Exactly how long she didn't know.

"Now dis peeshwank," Maw-Maw said when she lifted Matsi into the tub, "is special-special. My boys love de Asian, f'sure, f'true, and dis one delish." Maw-Maw wasn't always mean.

"Not everbody take chirren," she said. "Afraid of police, say you trouble-trouble." She slid her hand between her pillowy breasts. "Got big ole hawt, me. You lucky, dat." She pinched Matsi's thigh, making her jump. "Dumb as a turkey, ain't you? Could tell lies until daylight, me, and you wouldn't know."

Matsi kept her face bare of thoughts. She liked having secrets. When she was younger, she believed her parents knew everything

22

about her. That her thoughts jumped out of her head and tattled on her. The men who delivered her to Maw-Maw claimed she didn't understand English. Matsi hadn't corrected them, had acted ever since as though what they said was true.

The brown girls squawked like noisy birds when Maw-Maw wasn't around. Matsi ignored them and their unfamiliar language. She didn't want them as friends. They were dangerous, forever getting in trouble.

The day the wave smashed its big angry fist into Phi Phi Don, the H-shaped island that Daddy said must have been named by someone who stuttered – he was so funny, he made her laugh – they were creeping like spies through the tickled pink lobby. Their mission: find Mummy on the beach.

A loud swishy swoosh was all they heard before water swallowed the floor. They found a post to wrap arms around so they wouldn't be swept away with the lamps and sofas and see-through tables. Climb onto me, Empress, Daddy said, when the water reached his chest. Matsi did and a yellow car floated la-di-da by, pretending to be a duckanary. Pretending to be something special. That car had quite the imagination.

Maw-Maw held contests as many times a night as business demanded. "I'm famous f'dat, me," she said. "Down de road, up de road, from anywheres dey come." She dressed the girls in costumes, gave them make-believe names. They were the prizes, paraded one at a time in front of contestants on metal folding chairs in the back room of a barber shop.

The girls lined up behind a door to the contest room, Matsi first. "I give all my boys de same chance at de most exotic girl," Maw-Maw said. "I'm fair, me."

Peeking around the door, Matsi counted seven men. Maw-Maw wouldn't be cross tonight. When there were fewer men than girls, some of the girls weren't chosen, making it harder for them to earn back what Maw-Maw had paid for them. She kept a cigar box of poker chips for each girl. *Scores* of chips. Every time a girl went with a man, one of her chips disappeared. Once a girl's box was empty she'd be paid up and could go home for good. On a busy night, Matsi could make as many as ten chips disappear. But Maw-Maw added more each day for food and fines. Not being chosen got you fined so Matsi put on a show.

When Maw-Maw's smoky voice called out, "Pree-zen-tin," Matsi loosened the belt of her slippery pink kimono. When Maw-Maw clapped her hands and said, "Li'l Lotus Lady," Matsi pushed the door open wide. Maw-Maw held out her arms and smiled as if Matsi were her own. Matsi wanted to believe in that smile, wanted to run into those arms and lay her head on that great soft chest.

"Dis little boo from Thailand," Maw-Maw said, turning to the men. "Dey do great yum-yum dere, dey all do, and dis sea bob de expert." Yum-yum. The sound of the word made the back of Matsi's throat ache. Eyes down and hands pressed as if in prayer, she took baby steps into the room "quick-quick" as Maw-Maw had trained her. Reaching the center, she bowed.

"She doan say a word, woan hurt your ear," Maw-Maw said. "Just gonna show you and you gonna love it." Matsi dropped her kimono to the floor and pirouetted. "Who gonna win dis one?"

Voices called out while Matsi did ballerina leaps across the room. The tall, jumpy man with the shaved head and goldfish eyes called out the highest number. He'd won her once before and all he'd wanted was to play jacks with his clothes off. He didn't have stinky armpits, hadn't bitten her or made her gag and choke. Getting him a second time was good luck. A seed of hope sprouted in her chest.

As Maw-Maw brought out the next girl, a big show-off with castanets, Matsi scooped up her kimono and accompanied goldfish eyes to the winners' door. For the next thirty minutes, she would do as Maw-Maw instructed: "Don't be fussy-fussy. Don't ack like you tink you too good f'dem. Do anytin dey wants cept go-go. When you ready f'go-go, gonna cost more."

At the door, Maw-Maw's red-bearded son, T-Henry, put gold-fish eye's payment into the money belt resting on his belly shelf.

T-Henry was the timekeeper, too, and the one who made sure men didn't try to get more than they paid for. Behind the door three rooms led into each other like cars on a train, each sectioned off with sheets into smaller rooms trapping hot, sticky air that made the walls weep. Terrible feng shui, Matsi's mother would have said. And the smell. Like someone had thrown up fish sticks.

"Name's Lionel," goldfish eyes said when they got to their room. "Didn't tell you first time. Wasn't sure I could trust you." He spoke fast, using up nearly all his breath. "Then, I figured, who would you tell? You a working gal and not from these parts."

Matsi clutched the kimono to her chest and watched Lionel's jeans and briefs slide down to his sandals. "I love kids," he said, stepping out of his shoes and pants. Damp, dark hair streaked his chicken bone legs. "How could it be wrong to love you?"

She looked up at the red and blue letters on his white T-shirt: *Land of the Free. Apparently.* She liked to read, to learn new words.

Lionel pulled the shirt over his head, folded his clothes into tight squares and placed them on top of his sandals. He sat on the narrow bed and signaled Matsi to join him. Gripped the base of his penis with a trembling hand. "You can touch it if you want."

Matsi cocked her head and frowned as though she didn't understand. Lionel pointed. She nodded, complied. She always did just enough to keep a man from complaining.

"Why should I be looking over my shoulder all the time? It's a terrible way to live."

He covered her hand with his and slid it up and down. She kept her eyes on the silver cross hanging from his neck, watching it rise and fall until he was done.

They sat on the floor, then, and played with the pick-up-sticks he'd brought until T-Henry called time. Lionel looked older than Matsi's father, but he was better at games, able to pick up the Master Stick every time.

That night, as Maw-Maw said, "Time to make do-do" – time for sleep – her voice was almost gentle. Lionel was the reason, Matsi was sure. Lionel was a good luck charm.

*To the refugee camp, to the hospital, to the temple turned into
a morgue, they took their meagre offerings: Mummy's passport,
matted hair from her brush, her* DNA *which means Do Not Ask,
as in do not ask for the Empress of Heaven. She'll have to find her
fancy robe first, she'll likely show up late. For rescues, the Empress
much prefers Ma-tsu. If you call her that, she'll come right away.*

*To the officer filling out forms, Daddy said: She's light as a
cork with onyx black hair and eyes as brown as earth. Sounds
like scores of the missing, the form filler said, whole light-as-cork
villages gone. How many are scores? Matsi asked as she picked
at a scab. Too many, said Daddy, and he slid to the ground while
chanting monks barefooted by in a colour you won't find in a box
of crayons. The Empress would've worn red.*

Lionel showed up once a week, sometimes not able to win her
until the second or third contest. "I'd be here all the time if I had
the cash," he said one night, dropping his jeans. "Waiting for you
to come into the room, my heart revs like it's pure caffeine. Soon
as you dance, I calm right down. You smile so pretty, it's obvious
you like it. No one can say I'm taking advantage."

He'd brought a checkerboard and after he was done, they sat
on the floor with their legs open, the board between them. "First
game won't count because you're learning, okay?" Matsi had been
playing checkers since before she started school. It was spooky,
her father said, how good she was at it. She saw moves before
they happened as though they couldn't do anything *but* happen
that way.

"You and I, we're free spirits," Lionel said, pouring checkers out
of a plastic bag. "You want the red or the black men?" She pointed
to the red ones without thinking and her stomach went sour, but
his expression didn't change. Keeping her secret was easy with
other men. They rarely spoke to her. What if Lionel was trying to
trap her, was spying for Maw-Maw?

"The rest of the world doesn't understand free spirits. Seems
only Jesus can forgive. My mama can't. She kicked me out. I'll go
first."

He moved a black. The blacks were men and kings.

She moved a red. Girls and empresses.

"People think kids can't make decisions but here you are working already, on your own, so to speak. Kids are naturally sexual. Somebody famous said that first, can't remember who."

He moved a black.

She moved a red. Was moving a checker making a decision?

"Know what my problem is? I'm ahead of my time. Paying for this is baloney. We should be free to make each other feel good whenever we want."

He moved a black and she captured it.

"Shoot! How about I teach you English? Then you could tell me how you did that. It's terrible what happened to your people. I said a prayer for them."

Maybe Lionel was a detective her father had hired. If so, he'd probably expect her to look like her last school photo. Her hair hadn't been twisted on top of her head. She yanked out the rubber band and the plastic clips Maw-Maw put in each night, let her hair drop to her shoulders. Onyx black.

"Hey," Lionel said, "I was just thinking about your hair, wondering how long it was. Pop would've said 'quite the co-inky-dink.' Thought he was a real comedian, the bastard." His hand flew up and pressed his forehead as if he'd eaten ice cream too fast. "What a jerk! Cussing in front of a lady. I'm so sorry, so sorry. Can you forgive me?" He looked as if he might cry.

Matsi held out a clip that had retained a strand of her DNA. Lionel took it and kissed her hand over and over with his thin, dry lips.

She held her hand to her nose that night. No trace of his scrubbed clean smell.

A good-news-at-last story spread through the camp. While off on a beach, in search of his wife, a man found dolphins in a once dry lagoon that the dead had churned into poison. A pinky-gray humpback mum and her kid. They'd surfed over trees. Apparently. A miracle, a sign of hope like Ice Cream Next Exit. But as it turned out, just the mum got rescued. The kid must have called for the Empress of Heaven.

Between Lionel's visits, Matsi replayed his breathy voice in her head. She wished he'd never won her. The things he said – like, just because he was older didn't mean they couldn't love each other – made her loneliness worse. Her parents had said, "Love you" every morning before she went to school and every evening when they tucked her in. "Love you, too," she always sang back. She no longer remembered her room.

"Pop never hugged me," Lionel said one night, pulling Matsi onto his lap. His penis rose like a cobra between her legs. "If I went to hug him, he'd say 'quit acting like a girl.' He didn't respect my rights, either. When I was ten he gave my bike away because I forgot to hang up my clothes one day. Can you believe that? I mean, I was only ten."

Matsi squeezed the cobra with her thighs. Was this acting like a girl? Lionel touched her shoulders and back in little tickles she didn't mind.

"He didn't have my permission to give that bike away. Ma always made excuses for him – he'd had a bad day at work, he didn't feel good, us kids were too noisy. She knew that wasn't true. She was lying. I hate liars."

Matsi's throat went hard as a marble. Having a secret was no good if you could never share it with someone. Especially if he found out before you told him and thought you were a liar. She wanted to speak so badly she almost threw up.

"Sometimes when I can't get you right away, I sit on another man's chair after he goes off with a gal. I like the warmth he left behind. I mean if there's something wrong with me, same thing's wrong with him, right?"

Matsi didn't know what to do about the marble in her throat. And the tears that dripped from her face onto Lionel's leg.

"Hey, hey," he said, turning her around to face him. "Not hurting you, am I? I never want to hurt you." He wiped her tears with his thumb.

She knew Lionel loved her. It was her stubborn voice that needed persuading.

"If I could, I'd take you home with me."

Why couldn't he?

Daddy sent her away with friends of friends who turned up at the camp where you huddled in tents when you weren't collecting bodies. From Vancouver, too, they were, the Wongs. Quite the co-inky-dink. They gave her a gift with their claw-like hands, a miniature elephant carved from teak. They called it Packy Durm.

Matsi. Such a distinctive name, Mrs. Wong said in a voice that came out of her nose. After Ma-tsu, Daddy explained, the Goddess of the Sea. Also called the Empress of Heaven, Mr. Wong said, trying to wear the smarter pants. Astride the bribing Packy Durm, Matsi rode into the conversation: When Ma-tsu was born she didn't cry and neither did I. Her very first name was Silent Girl. How brave she was, said Mr. Wong. Precocious, too, no doubt. Matsi wanted to stay and play detective, find Mummy in a lagoon, but seven-year-olds don't get to vote. Daddy wrote to Whom It May that it was okay if the Wongs took her home to her aunt who would hug her, feed her, and walk her to school, like a puppy from the pound. It's safer there, Daddy said. Only sickness and sorrow here, only corpses burning on wooden pyres.

"Aver so often a charmer get friendly wit a boy, tink he help her leave afore she paid up," Maw-Maw said one night before the evening's first contest. She was brushing Matsi's hair, checking it for bugs that looked like sesame seeds when they fell to the floor.

When Matsi remembered not to twist her hair into knots as she slept, Maw-Maw rewarded her with tender strokes of the brush that entered her brain and hypnotized her.

"Case you tinkin dat way, let me tell you de police just gonna bring you back. Police and me take care a each other."

Matsi sat on a stool, her head and back cushioned by Maw-Maw's chest.

Maw-Maw tugged at Matsi's ear. "You know what I sayin. T-Henry seen dat boy talkin at you, de one wit a head as swively as a owl's. Seen him teachin you games. Seen you understandin."

Matsi closed her eyes as Maw-Maw caught her hair in both hands and cinched it with a rubber band. The briefest of memories skipped through her heart: her head in her mother's lap, Mummy stroking her hair and the side of her face.

"Never seen dat afore, me. A boy wantin the same twat aver time. Nuttin wrong wit dat. Good f'business, actually. He bid averbody else up, him. How much he gonna pay f'go-go, I wonder. You ready f'dat? Afore I pin you up, get down on de floor."

Maw-Maw lifted her off the stool and placed her on her back; bent her knees open like a frog's. She'd lain like that when Maw-Maw bought her, before the price was set.

"May be dipped in de bayou, me, but I know my business. When you make de boys wait f'go-go, dey wet demselves tinkin bout it. Bring all de cash dey got, happy to give it to me."

She stuck her finger in Matsi's hole and wiggled it around. Monkeys scooted across Matsi's mind, looking for places to pee.

Maw-Maw grunted, pulled her finger out. "Still too small. Could bleed to det. Not trowin you way like dat. I take care a my dahlins. When you ready, gonna be de best contest ever. Li'l Lotus Lady: de rabbit in a pack a foxes. Get dubba my money back."

Matsi heard nothing after bleed to death. She stumbled as she danced for the men that night. Stared at the older girls who did go-go. For the first time she wanted to speak to them, ask them what it was like. Wanted to kick them for not knowing English. Pound them with her fists for knowing something more important. Maw-Maw could decide any day that Matsi was ready for go-go. She had to convince her voice to trust Lionel.

A bus chug-chugged them away from camp, past shredded houses, shrouded mounds of bodies. Then one plane flew them to Hong Kong where the Wongs tried to pretend the next plane would go to Vancouver. Didn't they know she could read?

Mr. Wong said: Don't spoil the surprise from your father, your auntie, and us. Trust me, you'll love it, that's all I will say, the department of questions is closed.

A surprise to ponder while riding on clouds, earning junior pilot wings.

You're going to Disneyland, Mrs. Wong said, as the plane dropped onto LA which means Left Alone, Liars All. Auntie's meeting you here, will take you there in a big white van, let's hurry and find it, shall we?

Disneyland! Matsi ran with the Wongs but they found the wrong van and left her alone to flail at two men who tied her with rope and taped her mouth shut.

It was dark outside when the van parked beside a lonely house in a field of scorched grass. They carried her in like a bag of rice, flung her onto a mattress, and cut her loose to face the stares of a dozen girls from under the sea or maybe Pluto, so weird the language they spoke.

Matsi and her voice were ready for Lionel's next visit. Only a few men sat in the room, elbows on knees, talking to each other, paying little attention to her dancing. Lionel won her easily. He seemed anxious, said, "Hurry up," as she stooped for her kimono.

"Florida's evacuating," he said when they got to their room. He unzipped his pants. "Why aren't we? Nobody's telling us what to do. The governor says we should pray. That the best she can come up with?" His bushy eyebrows rose up and down like inchworms.

When he didn't pick up his clothes, Matsi lifted them off the floor one at a time and folded them into tight squares. Waited for him to notice.

"Some people say it's no big deal, we've had a couple worse ones already this year. But I know we're overdue for a reckoning. God is not happy with us."

His penis drooped like a used-up balloon.

"They say it won't be as bad as the big flood when I was a kid. All I remember are coffins floating down the street, giving me nightmares."

When it rained day after day in Vancouver, some people's garages flooded. Matsi had seen it on TV. She stroked Lionel's penis but it stayed soft. He pushed her hand away.

"Sorry, gal. Can't get my mind off the storm. Don't know why I'm here. Thinking of calling Ma. See if she needs help. Ever tell you I drive a school bus? I could get her whole neighborhood out of here on that bus. She'd like me then."

Matsi wouldn't take up much room on the bus, could share a seat with someone small. She yanked Lionel's arm until he looked down.

"What, sweetheart?"

She crooked her finger. He crouched in front of her, smiled.

She put her mouth to his ear and whispered, "Can you keep a secret?" Her voice sounded as if it had come through fog.

He sat down hard on the floor. "What the heck?"

"Shh," she said, pointing toward the door. "T-Henry."

"I feel really stupid," he said, softly. "They speak English in Thailand?"

"I'm from Canada."

He slowly shook his head. "How did you get here?"

Matsi spoke into his ear about the Wongs.

"Jesus." He pressed the sides of his head. "Means the cops are looking for you."

"I don't want the cops to find me. They'll get me in trouble with Maw-Maw. Can you call Daddy? I know the number."

Lionel grabbed his bundle of clothes and stood. "You're a real comedian. Can you imagine what he'd do to me if I told him I know where to find you?"

"Don't say your name."

He stepped into his shorts and jeans. "He'd trace my call, have me arrested."

"I'll tell him not to."

"You must've been laughing inside all this time, letting me jabber on, pretending you didn't understand." He finished dressing.

Matsi could see Lionel in his yellow bus, bouncing along with the bumps on the road, steering with one hand while turning on the wipers. "If you don't help me, nobody will," she said so quietly he might not have heard. The marble was back in her throat.

"It's like you were eavesdropping. I'm deeply disappointed." He turned away without kissing her hand, without promising to come back. She wanted to rip her voice out of her throat for saying all the wrong things.

When she returned to the contest room, T-Henry and Maw-Maw stood side by side. They looked but didn't say anything, didn't hit her for causing Lionel to leave before his time was up. There were no more contests that night. No more men arrived.

"Doan worry bout de turnout," Maw-Maw said later when she put the girls to bed. "No fines tonight. T-Henry gone to town, tellin all de boys bout our Hurricane Special. Next time you wake up, de place be chock a block with boys waitin f'you." Matsi curled into herself, thumb in her mouth. How long did it take to grow up and be able to punish people for hurting you, for making you want to die? If she were the real Empress, she'd hurl lightning at Lionel, banish him to the moon.

They laughed when she asked, Where's my suitcase, my back-pack? You're an actress, they said, in the game, now, no need for clothes. Smile for the camera, be sexy. See the others? See how they smile? One man cocked a gun and she smiled. The gun didn't get in the picture.

Look at you, a movie star, they said, making her run, jump, hopscotch on one foot. She shook with shame. It was wrong to be naked with strangers. They took pictures of men touching her, men clutching her, men sticking their fingers wherever they liked. Men rude as temple monkeys wanting only bananas, making you scream, Mummy shouting: Throw them the bunch.

Lionel had set everything off kilter. Maw-Maw woke the girls earlier the next day. Matsi was sure of it because her stomach wasn't yet rumbling. Maw-Maw hurried them through their baths, didn't fix their hair, didn't get them into their costumes, and didn't line them up behind the door. She brought them out naked and timid

33

into the contest room where eleven men stood around a radio one man held. Matsi tried not to look for Lionel.

"How all y'all doin?" Maw-Maw said.

"Storm's coming," someone said. "Get on with it."

"Yeah," said another, making his knuckles go snap.

"Okay, okay," Maw-Maw said. "Sit youself down, settle in real good. You face be red tomorra when dis bit o rain blow clear over de Guff."

No one sat. The air felt crackly, dangerous.

"You lucky tonight. F'one low price, averbody can have go-go wit all but two a de dahlin. May have to wait you turn, but nobody lonely tonight."

"How much?" one man asked, taking a seat.

"Hold you water. I gettin to dat. F'you boys wantin sometin to member dis li'l bitty rain, Maw-Maw got two contest tonight, each a one f'two dahlin never done go-go afore. Boat a dem tight as Chinee finger puzzle. You aver seen one of dem puzzle?" Maw-Maw put the tips of her middle fingers together and pretended to struggle to pull them apart. The men laughed, ugly laughs that made Matsi shiver.

Maw-Maw turned to her. "First on the menu: Li'l Lotus Lady. So tiny, a mosquito could carry her away. Well, maybe a big mosquito. Plenty a dem around." The men laughed again. A few clapped. Matsi hugged herself, ashamed of her nakedness for the first time in a long while. When the bidding started, she tuned out the noise. Heard only her own short breaths.

You're better than drugs, said the man with the gun. Can be sold more than once if you keep yourself pretty. Stop licking your lips, making that ring round your rosy mouth.

They sold her to new men who sold her to new men who sold her to house after house, each one farther away from LA, each one guarded by guns and slobbering dogs. You had to feel sorry for the dogs in that heat. Each house was the same until Maw-Maw's, the same boring movie star stuff. After a while you want more to do, when there's nothing to read, no one giving you homework.

Maw-Maw's was like skipping a grade, running to catch up on lessons you'd missed, especially the ones about go-go.

The man who won her had rat-like eyes, sharp little teeth, and three tiny jewels in the lobe of one ear. She stood straight as a pole when he dropped his pants. Still as a stone when he circled her waist with his clammy hands and lifted her up as if they were doing Swan Lake. He lifted her high and sat on the chair, spread her legs with his knees and speared her. She was somewhere else at the time, afloat by the door, which as it turned out, was a much better place to watch that poodoo ballet. Not much to see, the swan only screaming, staining the dance floor with drops of red rain.

T-Henry wrapped her in a sheet and carried her to the sleeping room where Maw-Maw waited. "Go back f'Rosie," she said, taking Matsi from him. "Gonna be awrite, Cherie," she said, easing Matsi onto a cot, kissing her forehead. She patted a warm, wet cloth between Matsi's legs where pain rose and fell like an ocean wave. Matsi couldn't stop her jaw from shaking. "Hush, Cherie," Maw-Maw said. "Hush, dahlin." Maw-Maw diapered her with a thick towel. Lifted and rocked her in her arms.

T-Henry came back with the girl Maw-Maw called Mexicali Rosie. Laid her on the cot next to Matsi. Blood streaked the girl's legs. Rosie cried like a little lamb. Maw-Maw lowered Matsi back onto the cot to tend to Rosie. She went back and forth between them – giving them sips of water, changing their diapers – for what felt like hours before the other girls came in. They stood silent around Rosie and Matsi until Maw-Maw said, "Time to make do-do." Said it softly, sadly. The girls went to their cots.

T-Henry's voice floated in from the doorway. "Ready, Ma?"

Maw-Maw slowly walked away, doused the light, and locked the door.

Matsi rode her pain for hours, aware only of the occasional vibration of heavy trucks on the street, loudspeakers calling out words she couldn't decipher. Rosie cried off and on. "Hush, Cherie," Matsi would say, stretching her hand out to touch the girl's cot. She slept for a while, waking to the smack of wind and rain against the room's boarded up windows. She ached for food, almost frantic to hear the click of Maw-Maw's key. Hunger became nausea as the pain returned.

Rain pounded the roof and the walls. It shook the house. Close by, the sound of splashing water. The others must have heard it, too. They were talking excitedly, feeling their way around in the dark.

A loud snap made one of the girls yelp. Matsi pushed herself onto her elbows and strained to see. A chunk of the roof had fallen through the ceiling and onto some cots. Water streamed in, filling the room faster than Matsi thought possible, lifting her cot off the floor, turning it into a raft that soon overturned. She tried to doggy paddle but the diaper dragged her down. She pulled it off and winced as cold water stung her wounded place. She bumped into Rosie who lay on the rising water like a fallen leaf. Rosie looked dead.

Matsi screamed and two older girls swam to her side. One hooked an arm around Rosie's neck and pulled her toward the ceiling. The other took Matsi's hand and did the same, making Matsi ashamed. They were braver than she. Stronger, too. They hoisted themselves onto the roof, pulling Matsi and Rosie behind them.

Matsi clung to shingles as the rain beat her back and her legs and glued her hair to her head. She couldn't remember the last time she'd been outside. The wind sounded like a plane lifting off a runway, perhaps a plane to Vancouver. One by one the brown girls flopped onto the roof and Matsi lay with them like sisters, their bodies a chain, hand locked into hand, those on either side of Rosie gripping her wrists.

As the wind and rain subsided, Matsi raised her head to a world like nothing she'd ever seen. Houses were drowning. Only rooftops poked out as far as she could see, people-shapes sitting or standing on them. The sole lights were tiny ones like fireflies blinking on and off from those rooftops. She heard a yell here, another there. A helicopter flew overhead and one of the girls called out to it.

The pilot must not have heard. Her back began itching, then her arms and her legs. The shingles in front of her seemed to move. The brown girls screamed. The roof was thick with bugs – spiders and roaches in search of higher ground. Someone swatted herself, letting go of Rosie who slipped off the roof. They all wailed then, making so much noise they didn't hear the boat. Who knows how long it took them to hear Maw-Maw and T-Henry shouting?

Balancing himself on the big-enough boat, T-Henry stood and held out his arms. "Crawl to the edge. I'll catch you." Maw-Maw sat beside him like royalty, her arms spread in welcome.

Matsi was sure the brown girls didn't understand T-Henry's words but they scurried to the edge of the roof and began dropping, one at a time, into his arms. One of the brave, strong girls helped Matsi up, helped lower her into the boat. Maw-Maw wrapped the girls in blankets though the day already was hot. She pressed Matsi to her chest.

"My poor li'l dahlin. I tell T-Henry, if dey doan get out, it meant to be. If dey do, Maw-Maw gonna be dere, gonna find nudder place f'dose dahlin, gonna start over."

As they rode away, Matsi thought about a park near her home with a hill she once loved to climb while her parents watched from below. "Keep going," they'd call out when she looked around, or "that's far enough." They weren't here now to tell her what to do.

She stared into the whirling, churning water. All sorts of things spun around before speeding on by – a sneaker, a plastic lawn chair, a dead dog poor thing. A girl could be swept away, too, be carried over rooftops and trees before riding a wave into a lagoon where someone looking for someone else would find her and take her home.

Matsi turned to Maw-Maw's bloated face, studied the eyes that never smiled even when the mouth did. She would not dance for that woman again.

Kesh Kumay

I see a woman may be made a fool / If she had not the spirit to resist.
    —Katherina in *The Taming of the Shrew*

CB&O

IN A YURT UNDER THE GAZE OF ANCIENT SNOW-TUFTED MOUNTAINS, Kyal huddles beneath a blanket, yearning to escape. Her father, grandmother, and younger sister sleep nearby.

It is quiet on the *jailoo*, the northern mountain pasture her family inhabits each May to October. She hears only the sheep calling from her uncle's pen and the occasional whinny from the horses hobbled in a meadow.

The greasy smell of boiled mutton lodges in every mat cushioning the dirt floor, every rug padding the walls, and every needlework bag and harness dangling from the slender birch spines of the yurt. The air reeks of unwashed bodies. It's tougher for Kyal to stomach, each year, after months away at university where she rents a room with a shower down the hall. She aired out her bedding this afternoon, spreading it over a carpet of wild thyme. She tents her nose with the blanket and breathes in the herb's sharp scent.

Dawn brings the smell of rice porridge and the rhythmic thump of her grandmother's wooden spoon against the side of the iron pot. An almost sacred sound Kyal has known since childhood, one that makes her feel guilty about wanting a different life, yet all the more impatient for it. She rolls over to see the woman she calls Ama, as if she were her mother, looking at her with eyes shrunken to slits in her wizened face.

"Oy," Dimira says, waving a hand in Kyal's direction. "Is it sloth you learn at school? Wake up to the sun of your ancestors."

Dimira cooks in a *kolomto* over an open fire. She could have a more modern stove but, at sixty-seven, she claims, she can't be changing habits for no good reason. Besides, it's the old ways the tourists with beeping wristwatches want to see, along with colourful attire. The first tourists of the season will arrive in a few hours. For a few *som*, Dimira will let them take her picture in her magenta turban, pink sweater, patterned skirt, and tarpaulin boots. She has taken easily to the country's move from communism to a free market economy. Embraced what the government calls cultural tourism: airplanes, Land Rovers, and convoys of bad-smelling Ladas bringing foreigners who seek a glimpse of a life they thought had disappeared.

Kyal sees her father, her Ata, through the open door flap, a silhouette against the rising light. With his two older brothers and their sons, Usen will round up and saddle the horses for the more adventurous tourists' four-day trek through a mountain pass. She appraises him as she would a stranger. He's fine-looking in his quilted jacket, cotton trousers, and black leather knee-high boots. An embroidered white felt *kalpak* with black flaps sits on his still-black hair. A moustache hangs over his lips like a horseshoe.

Kyal bathes in a river that's fed by a melting glacier. The shock of the icy water makes her feel superior to her family, more courageous. She braids her heavy dark hair and dresses for the tourists: ruffled black skirt, tight purple vest, and an imitation leather jacket from a bazaar at the Kazakh border. No one else around owns such a jacket.

After breakfast, she and Aigul set out in the thin clean air to find brush to supplement the dung Dimira dries for fuel. They follow the sheep road, bordered by edelweiss and dandelions as it was when they were children and more companionable, before the daring leaked out of Aigul. Her favourite possession is a plastic cola bottle a tourist discarded – Britney Spears on the label in traditional warrior queen gear as though she were a Manas scholar. Kyal dedicated a full semester to the Manas epic of struggle and freedom. Aigul studies nothing except Emil, an arrogant boy from another village.

Kyal pulls the wooden cart they will try to fill. Aigul takes short strides in her long, narrow skirt, hurrying to keep up with Kyal's stronger legs and deeper lungs. Aigul was born too early. Kyal can still see her sister lying in the hollow of their father's hand, can recall wanting to be small enough to fit there, too. She scarcely remembers her mother, but she remembers that.

"I went to the holy place the Monday before you returned," Aigul says, breathy already, her mouth wobbling around the words. "Emil took me. We piled up seven stones, ate bread, and said a prayer. I climbed the stairs without touching the rocks with my hands. I looked into the broken heart stone and made my wish."

"You must have been gone the whole day. How did you escape Ama?"

"It was her idea."

Amazing that Dimira would release Aigul for so long. She insists the girl spend afternoons helping her and the aunties make *shirdaks*. The women have a contract to deliver two of the elaborate felt carpets each month to a tourist outlet.

"Your wish is to marry Emil?"

"Yes."

"You run after that boy like a hungry dog. His head is already as big as a boulder."

"You could try to like him. Have you met anyone yet?"

There was one boy Kyal fantasized might carry her off to his rich America. But in cultural anthropology class one day he said her country was turning into a tacky theme park. "Yurt World," he called it and everyone laughed, filling her with shame. "I thought you were a good sport," he said later when she called him on it.

"I'm in no hurry to be a slave to a mother-in-law," Kyal says now to Aigul. She plans to be an ambassador, like the woman from Osh who wore a serious blue suit and spoke at the university about her posting to America. In daydreams, Kyal stands behind a podium before a crowd in a far away city, choosing just the right words to inspire respect and admiration for her people, keeping only a bit of the respect and admiration for herself.

"Was our mother a slave?" Aigul asks.

"She must have been. You see how Ama is. But how would I know?" Kyal was only three when their mother died giving birth. Aigul demands so little of the life she received at great cost.

"Emil's mother is kind," Aigul says. "We will work well together."

Kyal can see the married woman her sister will be – weather-roughened cheeks, shoulders rounded from making felt. Maybe it's the way she's begun shaping her eyebrows, but already Aigul's childishly pretty face has a worried look.

"Come to Bishkek with me in September," Kyal says. "I'll help you get a job."

"Selling vodka in a kiosk? I don't have the same choices as you."

"Because you won't take them! Come back with me. Give yourself a chance."

"I'm bound to Emil. There's nothing more to say." Aigul's wincing smile makes the dimple beside her mouth resemble a tiny incision.

"How will you like it with your in-laws right there, listening to you and Emil grunt in the dark?"

"Why must you be so rude? It won't be like that!"

"You think they'll go deaf when you move in?"

"We'll be quiet."

"Ha!" Kyal hates the lack of privacy in the yurt, wondering if the others suspect what she does in the dark, if they hear her quick, urgent breathing. What's it like with a husband whose breathing you can't control? How do you survive the humiliation?

"Ata is going to speak to you soon," Aigul says.

"I didn't realize he wasn't speaking to me. Just this morning he called out a list of things for me to do."

"About something else. Something important."

Kyal ignores the hint of despair in Aigul's voice. "Is this a riddle? I love riddles! Guess this one. The more you have, the less you see."

"If you want to get a husband, Kyal, you will have to sweeten your tongue."

"I don't want to 'get' a husband just like I don't want to get tuberculosis."

"At the holy place, I prayed for you, too."

Kyal flaps her lips like a horse. "Darkness," she says. "The answer is darkness."

"Ata will speak to you."

"Long noses" from the West arrive, laughing about how their van got stuck in the mud crossing a stream and they had to get out and push, the road the worst they'd ever seen with huge stones blocking the way. The trekkers, half a dozen punctual-looking Brits in riding gear, are anxious to be off, to see poppies on the mountains and, perhaps, a snow leopard. They're too late for the poppies and more likely to see a statue of a snow leopard than the real thing, but Kyal doesn't spoil their dream. Anything is possible. Usen brings out half a dozen sure-footed horses. Mindful of the clocks in foreign brains, he has his mounts ready to go on schedule.

The lazier, fatter tourists – a husband and wife from America and two Swiss sisters – will stay in separate guest yurts on which Dimira has posted hand-lettered "B&B" signs. Kyal's family gets 100 of the 150 *som* per night the tour company charges for each yurt. Most of it goes for university, so it's Kyal's job to tend to the yurts and entertain the tourists. She's done it for three summers and each year more visitors turn up. Able to speak four languages, she can usually decipher their requests. They come to depend on her, confiding when they find the food too fatty or the *koumiss* sour. As if she's one of them. She likes that.

Usen rides out with the trekkers a while, to be sure the horses behave. Kyal watches him get smaller, wondering if he'll keep his promise to be back for her first *kesh kumay* of the summer. He often stays away for days, returning inside a moat of sadness. She never asks why. So much goes unsaid between them.

In charge of the tourists left behind, she orchestrates the day to play to them, presenting her family as a tableau. First up: the making of *koumiss,* done several times a day while the mares are nursing. A cruel custom, a betrayal of the creatures Kyal loves. But not to serve *koumiss* is sacrilege, so she narrates while her uncles remove foals from their pen and tie them to stakes in the ground. Pulling against the ropes, the foals let out high-pitched *eee-ows* and *yeeks* that sound almost human. Their dams hear the racket and come down from the hills where they've been grazing. The tourists gasp at the frenzied mares heading towards them and turn to Kyal with panicky eyes. "They're not interested in you," she says.

The men allow the foals to nurse briefly before pushing them aside to milk the mares. In sheepskin *chanachs,* female cousins mix new milk with part of yesterday's fermenting in the warmth of the yurts. For the rest of the day, they will take turns whipping it constantly with a *bishkek,* the wooden stick the capital city is named after, until their arms and shoulders cry out in protest. Dimira gives the tourists cups of an already fermented batch. One of the sisters, her skin as white as dry river-bed stones, gags.

"Kyrgyz moonshine," the American man says and his wife laughs. Kyal laughs, too, as if she knows what moonshine is.

She never learns the tourists' names. Doesn't want to get so familiar they dismiss her as another of the simple herdspeople whose world they come to inhale. Let them report back that she is professional – sophisticated, even – in the leather jacket as black as a starless night. It will take time to become ambassador. She'll need different jobs along the way. If she makes a good impression, a tour company might hire her as a guide or an interpreter.

The afternoon is for horse games. Usen returns as if on cue, shimmering in the sun as he crosses the plateau. That he didn't forget fills Kyal's stomach with mortifying gratitude. He joins his brothers and nephews in *ulak tartysh.* Kyal describes it to the tourists as polo with a difference. The ball is a gutted, legless, decapitated sheep, weighted down with wet dirt. Each man attempts to scoop it up and keep it firmly atop his horse while charging to the goal line. It's a free-for-all that makes the tourists shout and gasp at the noise and the dust and the horsemen's skill. The danger is what excites Kyal. What she loves about riding. About living.

Next: her turn to make the tourists gasp and Usen look at her with pride. Time for *kesh kumay*. She fetches the sole white mare in the herd, hers since her sixteenth birthday. Aisulu. Beautiful Moon. The horse lifts her legs up and down in a nervous dance. Kyal closes her eyes and sucks in a breath before massaging Aisulu's shoulders and back. She takes her time. Lets the tourists wonder what is so daring that both girl and horse need calming. When Aisulu lowers her head and releases a deep fluttering breath through her nostrils, she is ready for the saddle.

Kesh kumay requires a young man. Kyal's cousin Almaz has been drafted for the part the past two summers. As family he's unsuitable, but family is all Kyal has. Striding the herd's black stallion, Almaz rides out with her to where Usen waits – some distance from the tourists but not too far to be seen. When Kyal and Almaz are in position, Usen shouts, "Go!" Knowing he'll give her a fifteen-second head start, Kyal takes off, whip in hand, leather boots straining against the stirrups, legs burning with ambition. The wind she stirs lifts the braids off her neck. Almaz whoops like a barbarian behind her. She imagines her father awhirl in her dust, lost in admiration: "My daughter; no one can catch her."

Tradition says if the boy can catch and kiss the girl, she is bound to fall in love with him. If he loses, she can whip him. Kyal was born to the saddle and has trained Aisulu to cover ground quickly. That her cousin might steal a kiss is revolting. She wins, as always, and declines to whip him. The tourists applaud her magnanimity. It's just a game but a deeply satisfying one.

After the race, the American woman says she heard most Kyrgyz brides are kidnapped. Kyal laughs. "No, no, no. *Ala kachuu* has been illegal since the Soviets took over. We're independent now, but it's still against the law." She doesn't mention that everyone whispers of someone who was taken against her will and that the police are too corrupt to enforce the law. Ambassadors aren't expected to reveal everything they know.

Later, as she helps with dinner, Kyal relates what the woman said. "Tell her to come to campfire tonight," Dimira says. "I will speak of *ala kachuu*."

Kyal can't remember a time Dimira didn't tell of the days when emirs and khans prevailed and people believed in flying camels. The stories are windows to Dimira's heart, the way she warns and protects and reveals what she sees inside others, the way she passes along lessons she fears have been lost. When Aigul and Kyal were little, Dimira fed Aigul tales of poor peasants submissive to Fate. Kyal preferred the ones about brave young women even though they rarely had happy endings.

This night, Dimira starts with a tale about a fox that learns there is no gratitude in the world. Then, fixing her eyes on the American woman, she tells of an old khan so cruel he killed one peasant each day. So lecherous he sent a gang to kidnap a poor peasant girl who lived with her father in a small village in a valley in the mountains. The girl was of indescribable beauty as all girls in Dimira's stories are. In a clear voice younger than her years, Dimira recites: "'I love another,' the girl cried. 'I shall not be yours.' She threw herself from a window in the Khan's towering fortress. From where she fell, caves opened up and pure, clean, crystal clear water flowed from them, forming the mountain lake the people call Issyk Kul. Only there do jagged peaks rise sheer from the water on all sides. Only there do hawks ride the wind and chase the clouds away."

Since Independence, Dimira has spoken only Kyrgyz. Kyal translates Dimira's words into English, trying to match her grandmother's facial expressions and gestures. English is better for getting to the point than for telling tales. Kyal has to be careful not to be done too soon or the tourists will think she's holding something back.

Two days pass before Usen speaks to Kyal as Aigul said he would. The family sits cross-legged on cushions, a kerosene lamp casting light on the meal before them. Kyal is blowing on her noodle soup when Usen clears his throat and speaks her name.

"Emil has asked permission to marry Aigul and I have said yes."

"What happy news," Kyal says. "Who would have guessed?"

Usen folds his arms across his chest. A nerve in his left eyelid twitches. "I told him my approval is conditional on you. As the oldest, you must marry first."

"*Erf!*" Kyal shoots back. "That's the old way, unnecessary."

"Don't scorn the old ways," Usen says. "We owe them our living."

"Some things aren't worth keeping." It astounds her that so many people believe Kyrgyz independence means bringing back the past.

"The Soviets mocked our ways," Dimira says. "They claimed we were backward. My mother was the last in her village to have a traditional wedding. It was beautiful, she said, everyone weeping rivers of tears. She drank from that memory as she dug irrigation ditches and waited for my father. He never returned from the war. I was five." Dimira wipes her eyes. She relates this story often and it never fails to move her.

"Who can afford such a wedding anymore?" Usen says.

"Emil's family," Aigul says. "They have many more horses than we do."

"Aigul will have to wait 'til I finish university," Kyal says, returning to her soup.

"You've had two years already," Usen says. "More than anyone in the village. We could better use the money on showers for the tourists and generators to power them."

Kyal's cheeks burn as if they've been slapped. She swallows hard and meets his impassive gaze. "I need a degree to get a good job."

"I sent you to find a husband. It's taking too long. Best you marry now and learn how to be a woman."

"I don't need to be a wife to be a woman."

"Bite your tongue!" Dimira says.

"Emil can't marry, either," Aigul says, "until his older brother does, and he isn't dating anyone." Her voice comes out in whining notes. She pushes her dish away, delicately, with the tips of her fingers.

"Perhaps the brother would be interested in a match with Kyal," Usen says.

"*Ahyee*, Ata, that's brilliant. The bride price you'll get for us! I am sure to fetch five horses. Kyal much less, because she's so bossy."

In classes, Kyal sits shoulder to shoulder with young men from other lands who don't expect her to lower her eyes when she speaks with them. Men taller than her father. Future lawyers and software designers who will live in houses with electricity, running water, and flush toilets. If she has to have a husband, she wants one like that. "One day I will go to America and come back with a groom," she says. "He will not own me for as little as five horses. He will not own me at all."

"He will be rich and carry a gun, I suppose," Dimira says. She saw a Hollywood movie once in Bishkek.

"I'll speak to Emil's family," Usen says, his voice unyielding. "I'll not be left with you on my hands."

Kyal gnaws her lower lip to stop her eyes from filling.

"Nobody gets to keep a daughter," Dimira says softly, squeezing Kyal's hand. "That's our way."

Usen strokes his face with both hands. "*Oomiyin,*" he says, ending the meal.

"*Oomiyin,*" Aigul and Dimira say.

Kyal cannot summon the word.

"He's afraid for you," Dimira says later as Kyal helps her wash the dishes. "Afraid you'll be like a river that wanders off and gets swallowed up by the desert. He hated giving all his hard work to the collective. Don't you remember? Our herds fed the entire Soviet Union and still they didn't respect us. There was a great forgetting those years when factories sprung up like grass. Some of our young people never learned their own language, their mouths full of the crude sound of Russian. Your father wants you to have the life he waited for, a life you reject."

"I don't! I'm studying it. But there's more in the world than this sliver of land."

"All your studies can do is to prove what we already know is true." Dimira retrieves a faded and cracked photograph from a chest behind the *kolomto* and holds it out. Kyal has seen this photo before: Dimira, her two sisters and their mother, standing in long dresses and coats, great gnarled mountains rising behind them.

"We lived on the roof of the world," Dimira says. "So high all we could raise were yaks. The sky and all that's in it came to us. Why go anywhere else?"

"That was a long time ago, Ama. Life can't be as it was then."

"It can. If there's only one road, no one gets lost."

Dimira hauls out tradition when it suits her. If she wanted to be rude, Kyal could point out that, in the past, selling things at market was considered a disgrace. Yet Ata sells horses and the women sell *shirdaks*. She studies her great-grandmother's face in the photograph. Gentle but unafraid. Loneliness settles over her like mountain mist. "What was my mother like?" she asks.

Dimira puts the photo away and takes Kyal's cheeks in her calloused hands. "Restless like you. Harder to hold than a green horse. It wore me out to watch her."

"Father never speaks of her. Why is that?"

"Because she was cursed. That's all you need to know." Dimira flicks her hands in dismissal and walks away.

Superstitious nonsense. A fantastic tale contrived to frighten.

The first batch of tourists leave and the second turns up, along with a young man on a high-stepping grey horse he has to rein in sharply. Kyal is outside grooming Aisulu. The man's horse is a natural racer, its body pulsing with energy. And oh, the soulful eyes – almond-shaped and hooded. Who chooses a horse so hard to control?

Aigul hurries up to her and whispers, "That's Jyrgal, Emil's brother."

He looks neither like Emil, whose features are too perfect to trust, nor like the American whose wide shoulders and straight teeth made Kyal weak in the knees. This man is skinny as a *bishkek* with a head so long and narrow, one might think his mother pressed it between two boards the moment he left the womb. The alpine sun has deeply scorched his once fair skin. A herder, Kyal thinks, disappointed.

Usen emerges from the yurt and holds the horse while Jyrgal – in jeans, long-sleeved black shirt, running shoes, and *kalpak* – dismounts. Usen calls out, "Kyal, I need you here now." He waits until she stands beside him before spitting on the ground, taking Jyrgal's two hands in his and asking, "How are your father's horses, Son?"

Jyrgal leans over to spit. "Strong and swift, praise Allah." His full voice is startling. Such a head should hold only thin, reedy sounds.

"Are you enjoying a peaceful life with your family?" Usen continues.

"More than I deserve, praise Allah," Jyrgal replies.

Kyal doubts religion rests any heavier on Jyrgal's shoulders than it does on Usen's and hers. "Praise Allah" is the polite thing to say, a ritual display she does not respect. She clears her throat in impatience.

Usen throws a frown her way. "My daughter, Kyal. The one we spoke of when your family welcomed me recently."

So he's done it. Sold her like a broodmare to this peasant. Tradition calls for her to bow slightly and cast a meek, virginal look at her suitor's feet. Instead, she thrusts out a hand to Jyrgal and stares boldly into his face. He's clean-shaven and smells like witch hazel. His eyes are as blue as a desert sky.

"My daughter likes to pretend she hasn't been brought up well," Usen says, pinching his cheek to show his disapproval.

His face solemn, Jyrgal grips Kyal's hand and pumps it, seemingly unfazed by her immodesty. Pretending. Or spineless. She pulls away from the hot pressure of his rough hands.

Usen leads them into the yurt where Dimira boils water on the *kolomto*. "My mother and daughter will serve us chai. Be seated. Please." He indicates the place of honour, the one he usually takes.

While they wait for their tea, the men agree that horses, not sheep, rule the landscape. Their voices recede into a crevice of Kyal's mind as she sets out cups, spoons jam into a bowl and slices bread Dimira baked that morning. She has signed up for field work the next semester. Travelling to burial grounds in search of ancient Turkic inscriptions. Unlocking secrets about the past. The yurt feels like her burial site as a pall of despair falls over her. Married women don't go to university. At least not women married to herdsmen. She looks at the straight-backed young man with reddish-brown hair as curly as a sheep's. Her back twitches in revulsion.

She sits beside Dimira and pours tea as Usen probes Jyrgal. He is twenty-five.

"Four years older than you, Kyal," her father says as if she can't subtract.

Dimira says, "Mmm."

Jyrgal's family breeds racers. "When I'm not tending the herd," Jyrgal says, "I train horses for the leaguers who play *ulak tartysh* in the hippodrome."

Dimira says, "Aah."

Usen says, "We play, too! My brothers, nephews, and I. You must join us."

"I will do that."

"Do you play an instrument?" Usen says. "The *komuz*, perhaps? Everyone plays the *komuz*, no?" He points to the three-stringed fretless lute leaning against a wall.

"No."

"Do you sing?"

"Like a mountain goose."

Usen forces a laugh. "That's a good one!"

Kyal steps in to save her father from further disgrace. "What, then?" she says. "You don't play. You don't sing. Have you no tricks?"

"I can recite verse," he says as if announcing he'd discovered a new planet.

"Un hun," Dimira says.

Usen says, "We would enjoy that."

Jyrgal stands and closes his eyes as though seeking inspiration. What a bore. Kyal would laugh if she weren't angry to the bottom of her heart at this charade engineered for her benefit. Ata knows all he wants to about Jyrgal. He has fallen in love with the idea of him. She is expected to do the same.

Eyes closed, Jyrgal recites, "Reaching with my right hand, I grasped the sun for myself."

Kyal strains to place these words she knows in familiar context.

Slowly, as though time belongs to him, Jyrgal raises his right arm to the roof and snatches at the air. "Reaching with my left hand, I caught the moon for myself. My right hand held the sun. My left hand held the moon."

He passes one arm in front of the other and Kyal remembers. It was in class. A reading from the Manas that brought her to tears.

"I took the sun and put it in place of the moon. I took the moon and put it in place of the sun. Together with the sun and moon, I flew high into the sky." He stretches both arms to the side and opens his eyes to a hushed audience.

"How do you know those lines?" Kyal asks, grudgingly impressed.

"My grandfather is a *manaschi*," he says, enunciating the words as though she were slow-witted. "I grew up with the Manas."

"*Manaschi*," Dimira whispers in reverence. "In the early Soviet days, before even I was born, *manaschi* disappeared like rabbits under tractors. Murdered or sent to Siberia. Later, when it wasn't so easy to make someone vanish without the world complaining, apprentices of the great *manaschi* came out of hiding. But they had to sing of a different Manas. No longer a warrior, but a working-class hero."

"My grandfather knows of those days," Jyrgal says to her.

"Did you meet him?" Dimira asks Usen.

Usen thrusts out his broad, flat chest and says, "I did." Stands and slaps Jyrgal's back. "Imagine! The milk of your clan and ours, flowing into the same *chanach*. Ama, where is the vodka? We must toast to Jyrgal's and Kyal's happiness. May they have many children running in front and many horses behind."

"I have neither received nor accepted a proposal," Kyal says.

Jyrgal sits beside her on the women's side of the table and leans into his words. "My brother is eager to wed and I am eager to help him."

"Do you exist only to serve your brother's whims?"

He straightens his back. "Helping a brother or sister is not a choice."

She matches his posture. "It is not yet your place to lecture me."

He narrows his eyes and says, "I'm reminded of hissing swans at Issyk Kul." He stands, extends his hands to Usen and nods toward Dimira. "Thank you for your hospitality. I won't keep you longer." Picking up his shoes at the entrance, he leaves.

Surprised at Jyrgal's sudden departure, Kyal doesn't notice Usen striding angrily toward her until his hand connects with her head.

"He has left the matter with me," Dimira says later after Usen packs his saddlebags and rides into the mountains. "He'll be gone a while. He wants a decision from you when he returns." She whispers because Aigul rests nearby. The reports of Kyal's recalcitrance have made her faint and nauseous.

"I have a say?"

"He was wrong to hit you. Anger and bitterness are gobbling him like cancer. But you don't appreciate what your ancestors endured to give you the luxury of speaking your mind." She grabs a bucket with one hand and beckons Kyal with the other. "Come with me to the river."

Outside, she says, "Before he left, your father told me you must agree to this match. He said he will not force you."

She must agree. Kyal mouths the words, imagining Ata's face as he spoke them. She takes the bucket from her grandmother and swings it wildly. Relief rises up through her body and erupts in laughter. She will not have to sacrifice herself for Aigul. Then she remembers that her father wants to spend her university money on tourists. She walks to the river with her head down, loathing the way her toes turn in.

Jyrgal shows up the next afternoon dressed for *ulak tartysh* in tank cap, high leather boots, and cushioned jacket. A sheepskin blanket protects his horse.

"Heaven bless you, you didn't scare him away," Aigul says.

He looks different to Kyal in the sun's heat. Almost attractive. But she'd rather make love to his horse. Ha! She is buoyant with audacity. When there wasn't the opportunity to decide, Jyrgal seemed as undesirable as any other villager. Now, she sees a tolerable possibility: marriage in exchange for a degree. She will convince Usen to forego any other bride price. He will persuade Jyrgal's family she'll be much more valuable property, later, when she commands a good salary and brings them prestige. "Our daughter-in-law, the ambassador." She'll need to stay in Bishkek during the school year, so there's her room and meals to cover as well as tuition. If Jyrgal insists, she will visit him weekends provided he doesn't disturb her study times. She can suffer his body two nights a week.

She watches him wrestle her uncles and cousins for the sheep's torso. Usen should be there to see it. Jyrgal brings the others' play to a new level. She rides past him as she heads out with Almaz for *kesh kumay*. Soon he'll know that no woman rides as well as she. He'll appreciate it, too, as the scornful American student never could.

An uncle officiates at the starting line. Kyal gives Aisulu an extra spur and leans forward until her chin is on the mare's neck. She's conscious of the sun lighting her jacket and the wind lifting her skirt above her thighs, of Jyrgal's eyes on her as she leaves Almaz pitifully behind, his war cries feeble in the distance. Conscious seconds later of the sound of hooves and the panting of another horse and rider at her flank. She turns her head to see Jyrgal no farther away than the length of her whip.

"What are you doing?" she shouts.

He draws up, blows her a kiss, turns sharply away and rides back to the laughing, cheering camp.

"I'll never agree to marry that horse's ass," she tells Aigul and Dimira later.

Aigul stamps her foot. "Selfish, selfish! Ama, what will I do?"

"Calm yourself, child," Dimira says. "You can't afford to get sick." She touches Aigul's head with an intimacy that pains Kyal. She no longer belongs to the world they so comfortably inhabit. Everything they do feels like a rebuke.

Dimira turns to her. "Before you make your decision, you will meet Jyrgal's family. We have been invited."

"I'm not interested."

"Then find a way to be. The grandfather will be there. You will accompany me to the *manaschi's* camp. I will not let you lose this opportunity."

In a rusty pick-up that transports their yurts from pasture to pasture, Usen's oldest brother drives Kyal and Dimira for several hours to reach Jyrgal's *jailoo*. It has only a few yurts, each made of white felt, not the humbler grey that suffices for Kyal's family. Satellite dishes rest on the ground. Here is a family of means, they shout.

Emil and Jyrgal stand outside in pressed slacks and sports jackets. Two men next to them wear ceremonial vests and *kalpaks*. One, an older version of Emil, must be the father; the other, with Jyrgal's long and narrow face, the *manaschi*. A white beard puffing like smoke from his chin makes him look mad. Was he initiated into his calling through a vision as it is said true *manaschi* must be? Kyal doesn't believe in divine intervention, but, sometimes, it scares her to think her destiny is in her hands alone.

As Dimira and Kyal step from the truck, half a dozen women surround them and hustle them past the men to the largest yurt where a well-fed, ruddy-faced woman waits between richly embroidered doorway flaps. She bows to Dimira and says in a voice as smooth as yak butter, "Welcome, Mother. I am Batigul," drawing out the last syllable as though her tongue is stuck. Taking Kyal's hand, she says, "Come, Daughter." Daughter? The other women follow them into the yurt where Aigul, a white scarf on her head, sits bent over on a carpeted platform, looking like a thief caught stealing the last of the winter hay. She does not raise her head when Kyal calls out to her in surprise. Spread on the floor in front of Aigul is a large cloth with loaves of round and layered bread, sour cream, dried fruits, and sweets Kyal has seen only on festival days. The strong, sweet smell of the bread makes her hungry. Is Jyrgal's family so wealthy they can go to this expense for all visitors? Batigul introduces Jyrgal's aunts and female cousins. "They've been baking and cooking for days," she says. "The men slaughtered a mare for the feast." She hands Dimira a white scarf like the one Aigul wears. "As we have no grandmother in our camp," she says, "the honour is yours."

Dimira spreads the scarf with her fingers and drapes it over Kyal's head. She kisses Kyal on both cheeks, but doesn't look in her eyes.

"Sounds of joy want to leap from my throat!" Batigul says. "Has anyone else ever been blessed with two beautiful new daughters on the same day?"

The yurt begins to feel small. The *shirdaks* on the walls press in on Kyal, their lurid colours screaming: Run! The scarf is a *jooluk*, a wedding scarf. She rips it off and throws it to the ground. Who are these women who conspire against one of their own? She stares at them and they stare back.

"She doesn't want to stay," says one. "She would rather be cursed."

"She will stay," Batigul says. "She knows it's an honour for a woman to be chosen this way. It's just that she is a virtuous girl whose duty it is to resist. Let us give her some time alone with her grandmother."

"My father will not permit this," Kyal says when all but Dimira have left. Her heart pounds and her stomach churns as though she were in the final stretch of a race. She steadies herself with deep breaths. She will talk her way out of this.

"He is not here," Dimira says. "The decision is mine."

"I won't stay."

"I'll tell you a story," Dimira says. She lowers herself onto a cushion and gestures for Kyal to join her. Kyal remains standing. Dimira sighs heavily and begins:

Once upon a time, not too many years before you were born, a girl of indescribable beauty was betrothed to a handsome young man.

Ideas scratch around in Kyal's mind like burrowing shrews. Dimira is in the path to the door, but she presents no challenge if Kyal chooses the right moment. By the time her grandmother struggles up from the floor, Kyal will be gone.

The young man worked long hours each day on a collective, saving for the girl's bride price, because she longed for a traditional, fairytale wedding. Not for her a Communist Youth Wedding! While he worked, he lost himself in reveries about the day his countrymen would be free to own horses again.

Lost in her own reverie, Dimira closes her eyes. Does she assume Kyal will stand still as a stick? An aluminum can sits by the stove – a large one likely holding milk or cooking oil. Kyal sidles over and nudges it with her toe. Full. She's lifted cans that weight before. She'll use it as a battering ram against anyone who tries to stop her.

The girl was assigned to a different collective. One day a hooligan she worked with kidnapped her, took her to his family's house and consummated a marriage with her by force. Later, when his parents relaxed their guard over her, she escaped, running for hours in bare feet to her home. Her parents refused to let her in.

'You have dishonoured tradition,' they said. 'Go back to your husband's home.' The girl was a woman now, spoiled, but she said she'd rather die. The young man who loved her took pity and married her. But it was too late for them. The women in the hooligan's family had cursed her when she ran away.

Kyal glances at Dimira, listens more carefully.

She gave birth to two sons who never drew a breath. Then a daughter arrived and lived. The couple thought the curse had lost its power. But when she delivered the next daughter, the beautiful young mother died.

Tears gather in great knots of pain in Kyal's throat. Two sons. Two brothers. Never a word about them, yet it is their absence as much as her mother's that hovers over her family like a thundercloud aching to break. It comes to her like a blow to the chest. She and Aigul were never enough.

The man blamed himself. If he had kidnapped her instead of indulging her foolish wedding dream, she would be alive today.

He would have sons to help with his herds, to sit with him on the honoured side of the table.

Dimira opens her eyes and gets to her feet with a grunt. "You have been claimed by a good man, Kyal. His name means gladness. Don't try to change your fate. You've crossed the threshold and worn the scarf. You are married to Jyrgal."

"You stupid old woman," Kyal says, not caring how much it will hurt. Forgetting the makeshift battering ram, she runs to the door where a wall of women blocks the exit. "Jyrgal!" she shouts at their backs. "Where are you, you coward?"

"Here," he says, as though dropped from a cloud. He bursts through the women, piercing the yurt, palms flat on his chest in apology. Dimira bows to him and leaves.

"Who sends a grandmother to steal a bride?" Kyal says. "Who have you recruited to rape me in your place?"

"No one will rape you. I won't force you to stay. This was Emil's plan. He was afraid to wait for you to fall in love with me. Desperate for you to take pity on Aigul once you knew."

"Knew what?"

He shifts his shoulders inside a jacket that looks a size too big. "Your grandmother was to have told you. Aigul is pregnant."

Kyal flushes with humiliation. She couldn't be trusted with the truth as Jyrgal was. She had to be tricked. Her stupid, careless sister! The tears she's been holding back escape. "Does my father know?" She picks up the wedding scarf from the floor and wipes her eyes.

"Aigul respects your father too much to tell him. If she marries now, they can say the baby came early."

Jyrgal takes the scarf from her. Has she offended him? She hopes so. She wants him to feel disgraced, too. "It's more likely fear, not respect, my sister feels. It's easy to confuse the two. Go take another woman."

"I don't relate to most women. You say what you think."

"Not a good trait in a wife."

"I think it is." He turns the scarf over in his hands. "Your eyes are so black, I wondered if your tears would be." He folds the scarf and places it on the platform where Aigul was sitting when Kyal first entered the yurt. He moves so close to Kyal she can see the sweat lining his upper lip. She steps back.

He places his palms on his chest again. "Sometimes I don't like what it means to be a man."

The bewilderment in his voice catches her off-guard. She touches his arm, hard beneath the soft, fine wool. "In Bishkek," she says, "I rent a room from a married couple. He drinks too much. She says there's nothing they don't know about each other, nothing new they can expect or hope."

"I know nothing about you," Jyrgal says, "except that you ride with wings."

"Your wings are bigger. You overtook me easily."

"I cheated."

So! Still never beaten. She's too pleased to be outraged. "What, Jyrgal the noble? Jyrgal the good?"

He gives her a grateful smile. "My horse is tethered behind the yurt. You'll handle him fine if you remember to still him with quiet halts."

"I don't understand."

"It will take me a few minutes to saddle another horse. When I come back, I'll say I couldn't find you."

Where would she go? Into the mountains? The desert? Neither village nor city offers refuge. Someone else would kidnap her. Someone without such an earnest face. She'd never see her family again. She drops to the floor, her shoulders and legs aching from vigilance. She wonders if a single fly has ever made it out of a spider's web. "You know the proverb," she says. "The earth is a small place for a fugitive."

"So, you believe in curses."

"No, but my family does. They would live their lives as if *they* were cursed."

Jyrgal walks to a trunk covered in brightly-collared tinplate. Such an unhurried walk. It must be how he keeps his horse calm. He pulls out a blanket embroidered in bold shades of green and gold. "My mother has been making quilts for years," he says, "to keep my future children warm. It's taken so long she's made enough for Emil's children, too."

Kyal will be expected to spew out a litter of sunburned faces and shaved heads, she supposes, each one taking her farther away from who she was born to be. "Your mother has an ugly mole on her chin," she says.

Jyrgal laughs from a depth that makes Kyal ache for all that has passed. For her mother who is now beyond all expectation. For the realization that when she left home this morning, it was already determined she'd never return.

"Can I really take your horse?"

"Yes."

"If not today, another day?"

"Yes."

"I'm not easy to live with," she says. "I'm not a good sport."

"I will try not to underestimate you."

"I believe in bathing often."

"Then, so do I." He steps toward her.

She puts up a hand to stop him. "We need to discuss the bride price."

His smile gives way. "Your grandmother and my parents already agreed to it. What are we to discuss?"

She tells him of her plan to become an ambassador. He listens seriously, nodding his head in a way she finds surprisingly endearing. *You've been claimed by a good man.*

"I can promise only that I will speak to my father on your behalf. If he agrees, my mother will follow. What about your grandmother?"

"That will be my test," Kyal says, "my first diplomatic assignment."

That night, the universe passes over the smoke hole in the yurt Kyal agrees to share with Jyrgal for a while, only a while. The moon, silent and lonely, peeps in through the hole. Kyal cannot see the Girl in the Moon, the orphan that the sun and moon rescued from a life of bondage. She feels the ground throb beneath her, feels part of an eternal flow of events. How many others in the world peer at the same moon? Unable to sleep, she watches the Great Bear slowly revolve around Polaris. Simply because it has chosen that path doesn't mean it's unable to choose a different one.

Deep Dark Waves

I, that please some, try all.
—Time as Chorus in *The Winter's Tale*

☙❧

SHE TOOK THE HAND HE EXTENDED AND STEPPED OUT OF THE CAR. When she reached for the baby, he said, "I'll do that. We need to get you in first." Had the muscles in her back and legs not ached from pushing Nicole out, had her anus not been on fire from who the hell knew what the doctor had done when she was spread open and helpless, she might have caught the treachery in his voice. She held onto his arm. Let him put one hand on her waist and guide her inside. As she hobbled into the washroom to change the soaked pad between her legs, he said he'd be right back. She didn't see him when she came out. The baby wasn't in the bassinet beside their bed. She shuffled to the garage. The car was gone.

8:30. Nearly sixteen years later, in a room with chandeliers and champagne-coloured walls, Sona prepares to speak of that day. The occasion is a breakfast to raise funds for several women's shelters in Toronto. As hotel staff clear plates and refill coffee cups, she stands in a shadowy corner, recalling how her lungs seized up in the forsaken garage, the simultaneous heating and cooling of her skin, the rage that lived in her throat for weeks, the months it took to resign herself to his having trumped her.

For shelters and community centres she dresses simply: flat shoes, a long skinny skirt, and a pastel sweater to set off her blue-grey eyes. Today it's a teal suit meant to say to the businesswomen she's facing: I'm one of you. Let me in. No matter how many times she gives this presentation, a gnawing at the base of her gut impels her to involve the audience in her grief.

Hearing her name, she sucks in her stomach and adjusts her skirt. As she approaches the podium, the room hushes. The women will be assessing her, looking for flaws. She carries no script. Leaning into the microphone, she begins.

"November 16, 1990, Wellesley Hospital. Nicole is born, arms and legs folded into each other. My Pretzel Baby. Nothing permanent, they assure me; for some reason she couldn't stretch out in my womb. Over the next thirty-six hours, I massage her limbs until they straighten ever so slightly and study the paper-thin nails curled into her tiny fists, unaware those are the only hours I'll ever have with her."

As Sona reveals the moment she realized Brian had taken Nicole and disappeared, a woman in the first row of round tables reaches under her chair and brings up a purse, pulls out a tissue.

Sona's amplified voice has a little girl quality she imagines coming across as both fragile and brave. In rooms with no microphone, she strains to be heard, especially in shelters where children keep interrupting their mothers. It makes her sound shrill.

"The police said unless Brian and I had filed for divorce or legal separation, he had the right to take his daughter anywhere he wanted. Being missing wasn't a crime. They said that in my own living room, as leaks spread like an ink blot test on both sides of my navy blue blouse." She sweeps her gaze across the upturned faces, smiles. "Always wear white when you're lactating – I'll wait a moment while you write that down." She pauses for the laughter, is relieved when the woman with the tissue smiles and settles back in her chair.

"So I said, 'Is *he* going to nurse her?' They asked if Brian had a history of mental illness, if everything was okay in our marriage. I said, 'What difference does it make if you don't find my baby?' They said I could go after him for theft if the car was in my name. It wasn't.

"My breasts were like granite. I pumped them to relieve the pain but also to keep my supply up. I was convinced he'd be back with her. It was unthinkable otherwise, unconscionable." A few women nod. They're hooked.

"After two weeks, I stopped. If Nicole was still alive, I reasoned, somebody would have put her on formula. Any of you gone through the agony of waiting for your milk to dry up? You could fly to the moon and back in the time it takes, right? I stuffed cabbage leaves in my bra – don't laugh; it works. I put bags of frozen peas on my chest, too, cursing my body for continuing to make milk for a lost baby."

Affection warms the cavernous room. Sona relaxes her spine. As head of consumer research for a marketing firm, she speaks with easy confidence to shareholders and clients on the proclivities of various demographic groups. Exposing her own life is different. She wants these women to care more about *her* than what she says.

"Just over a month later, on Christmas morning, I wake to new snow and a small white envelope delivered during the night through the mail slot in the front door. I stand on the chilly floor in bare feet and stare at it for a minute before stooping to pick it up. No postmark. A single white sheet inside. No greeting, no signature, eleven words typewritten on the middle of the page: *Nicole is safe. Adopted by good people. Private transaction. No records.*

"The police agreed he didn't have the right to do *that*. They alerted doctors to be on the lookout for Nicole and held a press conference in the frigid air outside police headquarters so, in a shivery voice, I could beg the 'good people' to give her up. My parents hired a private detective. Brian's dad offered a reward. You probably know all this. How many of you googled me? The whole ugly story orbits endlessly in cyberspace. Come on, don't be embarrassed. I would have." After nervous laughter, a number of hands snake up.

Sona googles Brian Patrick Warnock on Saturday nights when the stillness gets to her. She pours a glass of wine and sets up her laptop on the dining room table. In her profession, the prevailing assumption is, "If I know you, I can find you," but not so with Brian. In sixteen years, he hasn't used his credit card or passport, renewed his driver's license or the plates on the car. Searches for Nicole are equally fruitless. She'd have a new name, of course. Brian, too. Sona hounds the police whenever new fingerprint or DNA technology comes along, but they ignore her. In the early days when the story was fresh, she would get calls and letters: *I know where they are.* Sadists and nut cases. She followed up on them all.

Nicole is safe. From whom? How dare he.

Sona still lives in the two-bedroom brick bungalow they bought shortly before Nicole arrived, east of Toronto in what was then a neighbourhood of young families and retired couples. Her mother doesn't understand why she hasn't had Brian declared dead and sold the house, why she doesn't buy a condo downtown, something more befitting an executive. "Papa and I would feel like visiting, then."

Brian planted a row of cedars along the back. What a show he'd made of pulling gumboots over sweats and digging the holes, of ritualizing their new beginning. The cedars are twice Sona's height, now. Most of the older folks sold out to immigrants who've erected shrine-like multiple-storey homes. Something Sona would never have done back then. It was essential all rooms be on one floor. The new neighbours leave her alone. What song would you take to a deserted island if you could choose only one? *My Sharona,* Brian always said when they played that game, except he called it *My So-oh-na.*

A photo enlargement of day-old Nicole resides in the second bedroom along with framed letters, sympathy cards, and a montage of newspaper clippings showing Sona's young, anguished face. Nicole will need to know her history. Sona hung onto the crib and change table for two years before buying the twin bed and dresser – blond maple, European looking, not too little-girlish, even for a sixteen-year-old. She dusts the furniture every other week, changes the sheets once a month. The routine comforts her. Aspiring to move on is both hypocritical and futile, she tells anyone who brings it up. The best you can do is to layer one reality over the other.

Brian's clothes are on his side of the closet in their room just as he left them, shirts together and separate from the dress pants and sports jackets he wore to house showings, everything in descending order according to length. She wasn't surprised he didn't take the acid-washed jeans and Hawaiian shirts she'd talked him into. That he abandoned the rest kept her listening for his return past the point of self-respect. When dust settled on the clothes, she encased them in garment bags. Wrapped his shoes in tissue. Resentment still curdles in her stomach when she considers what he must have spent to re-outfit himself. He cleared out the bank account the day he left. She had to go begging to her parents.

At night, as the occasional light from a passing car streaks across the wall opposite her bed, she wonders if someone needing your forgiveness suffers more than you. She could pardon what Brian did to her but not what he did to Nicole. Or to their son. What restitution could he possibly offer that she would accept? She went a bit wild for a while, picking up men and bringing them home, convinced he was nearby, watching her. Thought she could flush him out. She rarely dates anymore. The nice ones don't move her. The others want to get rough too soon.

He hit her for the first time on an incredibly hot day in June, one that astonishes you because you don't expect such temperatures until July or August. They were living in Cabbagetown at the time and had just returned from a barbecue at Greg and Susan's. Another agent, Jake, was there with his wife, too. Listing out of Greg's real estate brokerage, Brian was surprisingly successful, despite his inability to hide his distaste for people who didn't meet his measure.

Sona had a few glasses of cheap white wine at the barbecue. She wasn't the only one. At some point she and Greg were standing shoulder-to-shoulder spitting watermelon seeds across the lawn, seeing who could get farther. It was a challenge to steer the slippery seeds with their tongues, to get them into firing position between their lips. With every spit, they sent each other into hysterics. Juice slithered down her chin onto the front of her sleeveless red blouse.

When she and Greg rejoined the others on the patio, Susan was serving coconut squares but Brian had his keys out, ready to go. He didn't speak in the car, didn't respond to anything she said. By the time they got home, she had worked herself into indignation over his unspoken rules about how she was supposed to behave.

"Plan on sulking all night?" she said as the door slammed behind them.

He set his keys on the foyer table and turned to her slowly, wearing his I'm-the-reasonable-one face.

"You can never say what you're thinking until the words are lined up in your head, can you?" she said. "It bugs the hell out of me."

"And we wouldn't want to bug you. So here it is. You humiliated me."

"I was having fun. It was a party, right?"

"Did you see Susan's face? She couldn't look at you, couldn't look at me either. Jake and Angie were so embarrassed, they couldn't say a thing."

"You could have joined in."

"You shouldn't drink. It turns you into a slut."

Still buzzed from the wine, she started dancing around like a boxer, singing *Heartache Tonight*. The Eagles. A big hit the year they met.

"I have to work with them," Brian said. "Does anyone exist in your world besides you?"

"The way you're going on, you'd think I humped him on the lawn."

He stepped forward and slapped her face so hard her eyes watered. She stared at him in disbelief for a moment then shoved him hard with both arms, knocking him into the wall. He twisted her arm behind her back, making her scream in pain, and pushed her to her knees.

"Shut up or I'll fucking kill you," he said.

She'd never heard that voice before and it silenced her. When he released her arm she swivelled to look at him. He was on his knees, too, leaning forward, his hands on his thighs, breathing through his mouth, a shocked look in his eyes. The air between them smelled different. Salty. Slippery. He entered her on the cold ceramic tile floor of the foyer. She climaxed so deeply it was as though a secret chamber had opened inside her.

In presentations she says only: "We were married a year the first time he hit me."

9:05. "I met him at university. He wasn't the least bit macho. Everything about him was orderly. My life, on the other hand, was as messy as my room in residence. My roommate was ready to dump me. I had never made my own bed, never done laundry or picked up a dust rag. My mother didn't trust me with her *Chatelaine*-perfect house."

As she looks out at these women she'd like to put her arms around, a memory of Brian slides across time: posture perfect on a straight-backed chair, reading and frowning, taking every word seriously. The frowning touched her once, that and his slippered feet.

"I'd never met anyone so methodical. He'd highlight passages in a chapter and outline those passages. Then he'd outline the outlines. I could only gaze in awe. I had no structure except my class schedule. Some days I didn't get up at all." She throws a smile around the room.

"I couldn't handle the freedom. My chaotic little brain was saying, 'This guy can save me.' And he did. He let me move in with him. Taught me how to find a ripe avocado and make hospital corners – fold, crease, tuck; fold, crease, tuck. Did you know batteries have expiry dates? I didn't. He taught me so much I never realized you even *needed* to know. His mother died when he was ten and, the way he tells it, his dad was hopeless around the house. Brian became the little housekeeper. What he wanted most in the world, he said, was a proper family. My parents thought he was perfect for me."

He was better looking than she deserved. Four inches taller. Blond flecks scattered throughout wavy brown hair never out of place. He didn't like her touching his hair, didn't like any impromptu shows of affection. His nose was the kind you'd sculpt if you were so inclined. That and his cleft chin.

"He's gorgeous," her mother said conspiratorially when Sona brought him home to Winnipeg that first Christmas.

"Except for his hands," Sona said. "Creepy soft." Her father's hands were wide and as sturdy as baseball mitts.

"It doesn't pay a girl to be picky," her mother said.

"*Hickety, pickety, my black hen,*" Sona said. She wanted to say, "It doesn't happen for me with him," but she and her mother didn't have that kind of relationship. Not until her second pregnancy did she conclude that genes had brought her and Brian together. Reading up on them, she became convinced they control nearly all human behaviour, that free will is a myth. Hadn't he admired her high cheekbones, her wide mouth? Their genes had wanted to mate. It was no more mysterious than that.

Now, at forty-five, the eggs issued to her at birth are down to a feeble few, or so they say. She's had to get reading glasses. But Brian's genes remain potent. He's only as old as her favourite photo of him, eyes behind the Top Gun sunglasses she bought for his twenty-sixth birthday. He wore them only the once, patiently explaining they were faddish. Some nights she leans the picture against her jewellery box and stands naked before it. She fluffs the black curls that spiral down her back and sends out telepathic beams of heat.

After her awakening, she expected it to be that way every time. Felt cheated when it wasn't and angry at Brian for being satisfied with less, as though that night hadn't happened for him. He went back to saying, "Want to do it?" before bed, applying Chapstick and switching off the light if she said no. He thought it was considerate, couldn't understand why the question turned her off.

She would goad him into raising his voice, into pushing and slapping her. She had trained herself to be reasonably neat in order to dodge arguments with him but now she wanted those arguments.

"Any reason why this dresser drawer is open?" he'd call out from the bedroom.

"No."

"I ran into it. I'll have a heck of a bruise on my thigh tomorrow."

"What a shame."

Or: "I thought we agreed to put our breakfast dishes in the dishwasher before we left for work, not leave them in the sink."

"Did we?" She loathed his cowardly approach, so like her mother's: *I thought we had an agreement, no lipstick until you're sixteen.*

She left her underwear on the floor. Stopped cleaning her hair off the tiles after a shower. He'd pound his fist into his hand or kick the base of the stairs, anything to avoid hitting her. Eventually he couldn't stop himself, as though he had crossed a threshold and no longer had any reason to hold back. The biggest rush for Sona came the moment before his face darkened and his eyes narrowed to slits of arctic blue. She would ache to be entered. The best sex was when he slapped her on the rear or choked or bit her. It made him so much more honest, so much more real.

9:15. Time for the part about the boy. Sona releases her grip on the podium and runs her hands down the sides of her skirt. She's irked the organizers forgot the portable microphone she had requested. She feels the need to move among the audience and place a hand on someone's shoulder, hungry for connection and the easing of conscience it might bring. She finds a person on whom to focus. A woman in a black pantsuit, leaning forward like a nervous friend, smiling encouragement.

"We had a child in 1985," she tells the woman. "A son." She can't bring herself to say his name. Sometimes she honestly doesn't remember it.

"We were renting a Cabbagetown heritage house, three stories of narrow rooms. A tunnel of a house, windows only in the front and back. The baby's room was on the second floor and Brian expected me to go up the stairs every time I needed a diaper, a blanket, anything. Great for dropping the extra pounds I lugged home from the hospital, but not practical.

"Another thing – I'm embarrassed to admit this: we weren't ready for the constant care a baby required. Neither of us had brothers or sisters and I hadn't been one to play with dolls. Didn't have a natural instinct. Each of us thought the other was doing it wrong. 'Don't pick him up the minute he cries,' Brian would say. I'd say, 'Keep your voice down. You're scaring him.'

"The bigger the boy grew, the more attached to me he became. 'If you'd show more interest in him,' I told Brian, 'he wouldn't always run to me.' But he and the boy were too much alike. They repelled each other.

"I got used to the fights between Brian and me. Didn't think much about them unless neighbours pounded the walls or the boy hid under his bed. For the longest time, it was mostly shouting, the occasional bruise I was able to cover up. I didn't think of calling a shelter until the boy was three and a half. He was so frightened, so miserable the day Brian knocked my face into the wall and broke my nose. 'Please, Mommy, can we run away?' he said. So we did.

"At the shelter they said I needed to start making 'healthier choices,' the way you might say: 'You should cut down on red meat.' Sorry," she says with a laugh, looking toward the shelter directors seated to her left at the head table. "The advice was faultless, of course, but I wasn't open to it at the time.

"Brian went ballistic. He phoned my boss and everyone in my department he could think off. You can imagine the fallout from that. I had told them my folks were in an accident, that I needed to make an emergency trip out West. I was too ashamed of the truth. He badgered my mother into spilling the beans. I hadn't told her which shelter we'd gone to, but he found us, anyway.

"He couldn't stand not being able to phone me several times a day. A shelter counsellor said that was controlling behaviour but I couldn't see it. From our first days together he phoned me wherever I was that he wasn't, leaving messages if I didn't answer, asking where I'd been when I phoned back. He was so crazy about me, he said, he wanted to know about every minute of my day. Nobody except my parents had ever loved me that much. Believe it or not, I used to kiss his shirts when I ironed them. He had to teach me how to iron, first, of course." She pauses but no one laughs. She taps the microphone gently. It's working. The room has become uncomfortably warm. It's the same every October. Hotels and office buildings seem incapable of keeping up with changes in outside temperature.

"He insisted on driving me everywhere just like my father who, by the way, still doesn't think I'm old enough to walk anywhere alone. At the shelter, they said I mistook being taken care of for being supported. Brian promised to go to counselling if I came back. The boy was so sad when I agreed. The shelter advised against joint counselling. They said Brian could hurt me later and blame it on something I said. But I promised the boy I would make everything better."

It took a while to find a therapist Brian would open up to: a narrow-faced man named Raymond who wore pressed jeans. He focused too much on their childhoods in Sona's opinion. So what if Brian was still angry at his mother for dying? Or that Sona's parents were a little Old World when it came to discipline? She wanted Raymond to make Brian stop upsetting the boy.

In the third session, Raymond suggested Sona was predisposed to violence.

"How did you come up with that?" she asked. "I've only hit him in self-defence."

"I needed six stitches after you whacked me with the hairbrush," Brian said. "The morning after you left the front door unlocked all night. Ring a bell?"

"You were lecturing me. As though you never forget anything." To Raymond she said, "He's the same age as me, but he acts like my father."

"Interesting," Raymond said.

"Anyone could have walked in off the street," Brian said, "cleaned us out, hacked us to death. We don't live in the safest area."

"Forgetting important things often signals repressed hostility," Raymond said.

"The door isn't the point," Brian said. "The point is: Sona hit me first."

"In our last session, you mentioned your mother smacked your hands with a ruler when you bit your nails, Sona," Raymond said. "Did your parents hit you anywhere else?" He made his fingers into a steeple.

"They spanked me, if that's what you mean. Parents did that then."

"Your mother or father or both?" He raised the steeple to his chin. She didn't answer right away. "My father."

"How did he spank you? With a belt, his hand, something else?"

"I don't remember." She hadn't thought of that for years, the wooziness as she bent over his knees, the sudden cold air on her skin, having to squeeze her muscles to keep from peeing.

"You don't remember?"

"No." Afterwards he'd kiss the throbbing skin and tell her he loved her.

"Did you like it?"

"I hardly think so."

"It's okay if you did. There's a thin line between pain and pleasure."

"Are you trying to say I like it when Brian hits me?"

"I hate losing control," Brian said. "It scares the hell out of me to think what I might do. I hit my mother once, just once, right before she died. A puny little kid punch, I don't even remember why. For the longest time, I thought I'd killed her."

Sona shifted sideways to look at his face – flushed from the effort of those words. For a moment, she saw their son in him. She reached over and rested her hand lightly on his.

"I sat at the foot of her bed after that until she died. Dad couldn't pry me away."

"Are you afraid Sona will die or otherwise abandon you?" Raymond said.

"Could be, I don't know. I give in to sex after the fights because she wants it, but it makes me ashamed. I'm tired of feeling ashamed."

Sona soundlessly opened and closed her mouth, lifted her hand off of Brian's.

"Giving in isn't giving," Raymond said.

"Stop," Sona said to Raymond. "Please. Just be quiet."

He did. She closed her eyes and wandered their house in her mind, touching the most ordinary of things: the stove top, the wooden ball at the bottom of the staircase, the bevelled edges of the stained glass in the front door. Sensuous things, and safe. It took her a moment to realize Brian was speaking to her. "Sorry?" she said.

"I said did I ever turn you on? Before this business between us?"

This business. If he hadn't blamed her for his feelings of shame, she might have tried to spare him. "Once or twice," she said.

"Once or twice," Brian said, so softly she could hardly hear him.

Raymond spoke of anger as a marauding general to whom they should never surrender. He sent them home with the directive to have gentle sex every day for a week. "Seduce each other," he said. "Try bubble baths, massages." Sona found it too contrived. They didn't go back to Raymond.

One day, under pretence of play, she punched Brian's arm.

"Ow," he said. "Cut it out."

"Mama hurt her widdle baby?" She flicked his cheek with a painted fingernail.

He grabbed her wrists and dug his thumbs in. "Why do you want me to hurt you?"

She didn't have an answer. Couldn't describe the craving that came in deep, dark waves that broke so gently at first she would get bolder and bolder, turning her back on the tsunami that eventually pulled them under. Coming up gasping for breath – alive! She wanted it again and again.

9:20. "Only once in a while did he hit me hard enough to leave marks. I never reported him so we didn't have a police file. The boy and I didn't make a habit of the shelter, either. What Brian did bothered the shelter staff more than it did me. They wanted me to take action, develop a plan, envision a new life, make a list of what I'd enjoy about it. Some women wrote things like: *Going to bed whenever I want. Rearranging the furniture. Not having to keep the kids quiet.* I couldn't think of anything."

Sona had a good position, even back then, tabulating consumer survey results and writing reports. She resented being lumped in with women who spoke in short sentences and used poor grammar, who needed to be coached through fire and safety drills. Some of them just had to tell everything, had to get every last piece of their pitiful stories out. A nunnery couldn't have been worse.

Sona fixes her gaze on the woman in black, on her short, blond hair caught in a spray of chandelier light. "Not long after his fourth birthday, the boy fell down the stairs and snapped his neck. He lived only three more days." The woman closes her eyes. Sona stops to clear her throat. She reaches for the water glass beside the podium, takes a drink.

She doesn't mention she and Brian were arguing on the landing outside the boy's room and the child ran out to protect her. That he threw his skinny little arms around Brian's legs and said, "Bad boy!" And that Brian pushed him away, causing him to tumble backwards down the stairs. She doesn't try to keep those memories alive. Watching him fall, rushing down after him, Brian stopping her from phoning for help right away, panicky over what she would say. Even now there's an unreal quality to that scene, like something she read about long ago.

They agreed to tell the paramedics, then later the police, it was an accident – that the boy had tripped over a toy. No one would suspect. Her visits to the shelter had been confidential. The neighbours had never called the cops on them. Brian placed a Tonka dump truck on the landing and tipped it on its side while Sona kneeled by the boy at the bottom of the stairs until the ambulance arrived, stroking his cheek, saying, "It's okay, it's okay, it's okay." She dared not hold him and make his injuries worse, didn't know it wouldn't have mattered.

When they moved to the bungalow, she shredded all photos of him, disposed of his clothes, his toys, and his bedroom furniture. In the lull before sleep finally takes her, she often sees his pinched eyes and worried mouth. He would have been twenty-two by now. Out of university or maybe going on for a graduate degree. He'd been bright enough, walking and talking early. Did her pretzel baby have difficulty learning to walk? Had she needed leg braces?

For nearly a year Sona and Brian constructed separate lives on the surface of what went unsaid and the secret they shared. He'd leave early and return late each day. She'd listen for the click of the front door as she lay awake in the boy's room where she took to sleeping after the funeral. She began studies toward a graduate degree, finding refuge in the evening and weekend classes, the assignments. She didn't ask where Brian had his meals. When they found themselves in the same space in the house, they were civil. Fine, thanks. Yes, thanks. Pardon me. They begged off when friends invited them out and eventually people left them alone.

He came to her one night after a storm knocked out the power, the heat.

"You cold?" he said.

"Yeah," she said, opening the duvet to him. She'd been off the pill for months.

9:30. "It took me a long time to say, 'Enough already.' It took me getting pregnant again. Brian exploded when I told him, said no way the baby was his. He claimed he'd had a vasectomy a few months after the boy died. When he eventually admitted he'd lied about that to see how I'd react, I said, 'You need serious help.' He said, 'You know dick all.' I laughed because he hardly ever said things like that. He didn't appreciate my sense of humour. I ended up with three broken ribs. It's a miracle I didn't miscarry.

"The shelter helped me apply for a restraining order and find a place to stay. If that had been the end of it, I wouldn't be in front of you today. But Brian was so shaken he enrolled in anger management therapy. He apologized over and over, said he'd care for the baby so I could get back to work sooner. He was always supportive of my career, I'll give him that. He promised he'd never hit me again. There seemed to be no good reason not to go back." She smiles ruefully. "I know, I know. How stupid can you get? I realize now that he didn't intend to change. He wanted revenge."

The woman in black frowns and sits back in her chair as though she's been shot. A surge of rage catches Sona off-guard, making her first hot then cold. The woman reminds her of someone hateful, she can't remember who. The impression is almost psychic. She's weary all of a sudden, almost too tired to go on. But she's expected to talk up the good work of shelters in support of the contribution pitch. And she does, barely hearing her own words until the merciful end: "What happened to me can happen to you. I tell my story so you won't ever have to tell yours." Applause enters her ears as static and the moderator appears from nowhere to stand beside her.

"For the generosity of your time," the woman says into the microphone, handing Sona an elegant blue box with brass hinges and clasp. Inside, a silk-lined groove cradles a delicate crystal hourglass. That someone might have chosen it specifically for her makes her feel both honoured and violated. She mumbles her appreciation and exits the room as quickly as dignity allows. On the way to the subway, she phones her assistant to say she won't be back in the office today.

11:20. The house smells of citrus plug-in air fresheners. Brian would be impressed at how housewifey she is now, how attentive to details that once bored her. She gets the eaves troughs cleaned out twice a year, the fireplace every two years. The roof was re-shingled five years ago. She opens a bottle of expensive red wine and leaves it to breathe while she changes into jeans and sweater. There was a time she couldn't uncork a bottle without making a mess of it.

She carries her glass and the blue gift box over to the window and sits in the wingback chair she bought for nursing Nicole. For a few minutes she watches leaves swirl in an autumn gust, their street dance mocking her mood. She's often depressed this time of year. She took drugs for it once upon a time but they made the pain too remote for too long. She prefers the more temporary effect of wine.

She was the one who was supposed to leave with Nicole. After a few months, once she and the baby were strong enough. She had played along with Brian partly out of compassion, partly to give herself more time. He'd been all lovey-dovey during her long labour, rubbing the small of her back, spooning ice chips into her mouth. It gave her pause, made her wonder if maybe they *could* start over. When he said, "This one's mine," as he held Nicole in the delivery room, she didn't hear the intent in the words. She just thought about the boy and felt wounded on his behalf.

She lifts the crystal hourglass out of its groove and turns it carefully. Tiny white grains of sand rush from one end to the other, completing their journey in seconds. She turns it again more slowly, hoping to capture the instant each shift in time begins.

The phone rings once and stops. She puts the hourglass back in the box. A few minutes later the phone rings again. She hurries to the kitchen to answer it. Whoever it was has hung up. Brian, she's sure, relying on nothing but instinct, a premonition from early morning that this day would be singular. And it has been. If the woman in black hadn't so unnerved her, she might have gone to the office. She was meant to come home, to receive his call. She leans against the refrigerator and stares at the phone, willing it to ring again.

Nicole is with me, he'll say. Age will have lowered his voice but she'll recognize it. *I never gave her up. I couldn't have done that. I just wanted to get you off our trail. I told her you were dead. That was terrible, I know.* He'll pause. *You still there?*

Yes, she'll say, already adrift in deep, dark waves.

She's asking questions I can't answer, now. She needs to know the truth.

After a brief silence during which he'll think she's absorbing the shock, she'll say something that conveys gratitude and understanding. Something to make him feel safe enough to continue.

Maybe they'll speak about that day and all the days since, what has happened in the world, how many more things there are to fear. She'll tell him she's a vice president and has him to thank for it, in a way – all those years free of distraction, all those years to devote to work. He'll tell her how he came to type out the note he left that Christmas Day, how he waited until the house was dark to pass it through the slot. She'll remind him the house is still half his, the property worth quite a bit more thanks to the immigrant shrines. He'll tell her who took them in – she won't care if it was another woman – and how scared he was that Nicole would die without Sona's milk. How regretful he's been every day since. She'll tell him his father retired last year, spends six months in Arizona and never gives up hope of hearing from his son. Should he mention reconciliation, she'll say there's plenty of time to talk about that later.

She retrieves her wine glass from the living room and hoists herself onto the kitchen counter. Sits and smiles at her legs, dangling like those of a ventriloquist's dummy. She studies the raised veins on her hands. After a while, she pulls out an open box of Triscuits from the cabinet above and finishes them off. Pours more wine. At dusk, she gets down and flicks on the overhead light. In the sudden illumination, it comes to her who the woman in black reminded her of: the director of the shelter she and the boy went to. The one who had spilled over with kindness the first few times, making Sona cups of tea, frowning with concern over her predicament. The one whose manner turned brusque and whose eyes turned cold the last time Sona agreed to go back to Brian.

"You don't seem interested in writing a happy ending for yourself," she'd said.

If Sona knew where that woman was today, she'd look her up, lean into that sanctimonious face and get right to the point. "I've spent sixteen years writing my story," she'd say, "and it *has* no ending."

Nobody; I Myself

Emilia: O, *who hath done this deed?*
Desdemona: *Nobody; I myself.*

—Othello

C3 80

I AM NOT A VICTIM. YOU'RE NOT TO FEEL SORRY FOR ME.

Feel sorry for Joe, whoever you are; speak out for him, please.

I try to stay on my side of the bed but sometimes I drift and his hands find my neck and squeeze it so hard I nearly swallow my tongue. His eyes are full of such fear and loathing you'd think I'm the enemy come clear across the world to take him out. He's sorry when he comes to, hates himself for the bruises he leaves.

Nearly six months since he returned but the nightmares don't quit. Ever try getting through to the VA? A waste of time. If he'd come back with no legs, they'd have him in rehab. He'd flip if he knew I made those calls.

Our only friend these days is Brother Darnell as he calls himself; no help at all.

He was over again last night, cranking the ancient bell – *brang, brang,* schmoozing our landlady, Mrs. Will. I can't hear what he says but I feel the smarm in his words. Slow as a cellar snake in winter, he climbs the warped, wooden stairs to the rooms we rent, scraping his shoes, driving me crazy with the urge to nail the swollen door shut. He no longer knocks. Says, hey, brother, how you feeling, before taking over the sagging horsehair couch, making points like a preacher, as if what he has to say can save Joe from the shivering sweats. I'm supposed to disappear when he arrives, hover in the kitchen in case their cups need filling.

Brother D – I call him that because it ticks him off – wears the same outfit every time: white drip-dry shirt, black rayon pants, and a thin black tie that buckles on his caved-in chest. Except for a halo of bushy hair, he's boring to look at.

The colored boys at school weren't boring, dressing like Sunday every day in vests and bright jackets and fedoras with feathers, bopping down the halls, laughing and calling out to the popular girls. Mocking us, it feels like now, daring us to be sluts. But who were they supposed to date if not us? Sixteen colored boys in my graduating class. Only four girls, names I can't remember, who hated themselves so much they bleached their skin and conked their hair.

Twenty out of 277 in my class and my mother thought they were taking over. Why do they have so many children? she says. Reads about Samoan tribes in *Ladies' Home Journal* but is not the least bit curious about anyone in our own country who doesn't look like her. Hangs up on me. It hurts less if I think of her as Faye.

I'm on lunch, writing in a closet customers use to open their safety deposit boxes in private. Stuffed what I wrote yesterday into an envelope and hid it in the drawer with the savings bonds, but I'm not sure if I want Earl – he's the head teller – finding it if I don't show up one day. Earl intends to be president of the bank one day, no humility about him at all.

Joe's on the new G.I. Bill, hundred bucks a month for going to school, taking mechanical drawing because, as he says, ha ha, there are way more jobs doing that than bayonet-sharpening. He could have gone to college three years ago on a football scholarship but it wasn't a full boat and he couldn't come up with the rest. It bothers me that he lets Brother D take up so much of his time; he could blow this chance to get out, to be somebody. At nine last night, I came into the front room and stood over him as he sat cross-legged at Brother D's feet, thighs straining against the fatigue pants he insists on wearing even though he didn't re-enlist. He looked miles away, untouchable. Hey, Marine, I said, trying to keep it light, school tomorrow, time to wrap it up. Without even looking, he waved me away.

Brother D rocked back on his skinny butt and laughed. To have a white woman who wasn't the town whore, he said, used to mean something. Joe stayed silent, just gazing into emptiness. Stand up for me, I wanted to say, but it would have put him in a bad spot. He's too kind-hearted to tell anyone off.

Brother D turned up a couple months ago with talk of an underground militia of colored vets. He was Lance Corporal Darnell Natson when he and Joe served together near Da Nang, getting high like everyone else to forget where they were. Joe thought Brother D was putting him on at first when he said he quit smoking and drinking so LBJ would have less tax money for killing. He wants Joe to go to Newark with him and teach the brothers there how to fight, brought it up again last night.

None of that turn-the-other-cheek, We Shall Overcome crap, he said. What'd it get for King and the brothers in Chicago? Bottles and rocks, that's what, and rotten eggs, don't forget the eggs. Shit, what a waste. Needed you and me there to take the enemy out, brother, play Bong the Cong. Gotta bring down the cities to make Whitey pay attention.

I try not to take that Whitey crap personally. If you suck up any more of that anger, I told Joe once we were alone, it'll poison you. What I loved about Joe even before I loved him was his detachment. Where is it now? When he says, right on, or I hear you, after one of Brother D's rants, I want to barf.

He's got nobody else to talk to, Joe said, least not anybody who knows what he went through, how disappointed he is. Thought people would shake his hand and say, thanks for risking your life for me. Thought they'd see he'd become a man. Back in The World he's still a nigger, a boy. Angry's his way of grieving.

What about you, I asked, are you grieving?

Oh, yeah.

I waited, but he didn't say more. I don't know when to press, when to let him be.

We need someone else over for a change. My best friend Natalie was home from college all summer and she didn't come, said she felt funny, why couldn't Joe and I have just shacked up instead of offending people by making it legal? I told her to bring Carol if she needed support – the three of us used to have a blast – and she said okay but it never happened.

We were watching a new show about space travel last night, holding hands on the couch, first time in ages, when Brother D arrived. Thought he'd be pleased to see a colored woman playing something other than a maid, but it got him so agitated he switched off the set like he owned it.

What's up, man? Joe said.

Where's her pride? Brother D said, pacing the room, stabbing the air with a finger. Can't go at our women on the plantation anymore, so they put a high yellow one on TV in a skirt cut up to her snatch. Bunch of crackers be jacking off tonight.

What plantation did you live on? I asked.

How about some coffee? Joe said, – then, as I left the room, Darnell, why you got to start trouble?

Look in the mirror, Brother D said, your green eyes, the red streaks in your hair. Pollution, brother, from the rape of your mama's great-great-grandma by a slave master.

Joe laughed so deeply it warmed my heart. He said, you been looking up my family tree? and Brother D said, don't need to. Your last name says it all. No self-respecting tribesman would have a slave owner name like Huff, Natson neither. That's why, people ask me, I tell them I got no last name, it was stole from me. I tell them something else they didn't learn in Sunday School: Adam and Eve was black.

That a fact? Joe said, still laughing, making me grin out there in the kitchen, making me feel almost confident.

Can't get a black person from a white one, Brother D said, because the white gene is recessive. Except he said ree-cessive, bugging me the same way the guy on the blues station bugs me when he says, listen up now, brothers an' sisters, hop in you Cadulac an' get you'self on down to Ray-moan Boulevard for some fresh futes and vedge-a-ta-bles. That's not a New Jersey accent. It just makes colored people more difficult to accept, screws everything up for Joe and me.

Anyway, the whole Adam and Eve thing is baloney, so I called out from the kitchen: If everyone came from just one man and one woman and they were colored – excuse me, black – where did that ree-cessive white gene come from?

Brother D scraped his way to the kitchen door, crossed his arms, and tried to stare me down. I stuck out my tongue. You got no respect, he said, and that's your man's fault. He looked over in Joe's direction. A man's gotta control his woman.

Joe went to bed right after Brother D left, then nearly strangled me around midnight, frustrating the hell out of me. I had to get up for work this morning, for crying out loud. How are we supposed to get by if I'm too tired for work or lose my voice? I kicked and punched him until he woke up and rolled off me, trembling so bad it scared me more than the choking.

They played Russian roulette with us, he said. Sent us on peace patrol into villages where snipers and five- and six-year-olds with grenades waited to knock us off one at a time. Never knew when your day would come up. It psyched me out, girl, called up something dangerous in me, something mean. We weren't supposed to fire on anyone, but I did.

(Like there's a fair way to fight a war.) You had to, I said, it was either you or them. You have nothing to be ashamed of. I couldn't bear to ask if he'd killed a child.

Darnell says we should have refused to go over there, Joe said, refused to exterminate those people like the government's trying to exterminate us, says we been brainwashed. I don't know who's screwing us over anymore, who isn't.

From Vietnam, Joe sent me a photo of himself cleaning a rifle, smiling, looking relaxed. I saw dreadful scenes in the papers but could never picture him in anything worse than a camp with bad weather where mortars flashed like holiday fireworks.

I pulled him to me and rubbed his head, something that usually turns me on – the prickly crew cut against my palm, the spicy smell floating up from his scalp – but slumping against my chest, he was a little boy needing to be held. Trust in us, I said, trust in you and me.

I wouldn't be with Joe today if not for the Conference of Christians and Jews the summer before my senior year. The faculty chose Sarah Silverstein and me to represent our school; I was the Christian, she the Jew. Busloads of us arrived at a campground bigger than a football field. We saw a film about a Negro couple who couldn't rent the apartment they wanted in New York City. (Everyone thinks this stuff happens only in the South, but look at Joe and me, stuck on Haydock Street and lucky to get in only because Mrs. Will remembered Joe from his varsity days. He was in the paper a lot then.) I was so humiliated for that couple it made me ashamed to be white – or, more accurately, yellowish pink, this black/white thing a pet peeve of mine. I'd describe Joe as kind of pecan; Brother D, the color of soot.

Every day, groups of us sat in circles on the ground, except for a girl from the Bronx with great thigh muscles who crouched like a Vietnamese peasant. We talked about fear and hate and the power they have. One night, we were hanging around the canteen, drinking sodas, someone playing guitar. A boy from my group and I were so hyped about what we'd discussed that day, we couldn't let it go. When the lights flashed at 10:30 for the girls' curfew, we were still at it.

I'll walk you to your cabin, he said, and we went hand-in-hand, talking so intently, nothing else mattered. I can't tell you that boy's name or if his hand eventually got warm and sticky in mine, that's how focused I was on what we were saying, how focused I was on his mind. Only when I got inside the cabin did I realize he was Negro. For the first time ever I'd been unconscious of color. You might say, big whoop or, disgusting. I don't know who you are, so I don't know what you'd say. It was the most amazing moment in my life. I must've looked looped, bouncing from girl to girl, sharing my revelation.

You're crazy, Sarah said – she who was in love with a Catholic who wanted to be a priest. Anyway, when I got back and my parents picked me up at the bus station, it was the first thing I told them. Imagine, I said, if the whole world could hold hands like that; if everyone, when they had to fill out a form and say what race they were, wrote down Human.

I was in the back seat of the car, my folks in the front, and they exchanged a look that said: I told you we shouldn't have let her go, next thing you know she'll be bringing one home.

When Joe and I eloped, they went into mourning, holing up in the house with the shades down for a good two weeks. Part of it, I'll admit, was the shock of not knowing anything about him, not knowing we'd written to each other for over a year.

You'll burn in Hell for your selfishness, Faye said, when I called from a motel on Route 1 to say I wouldn't be home for a few days.

You never think things through, my father got on the phone to say. Where are you going to live? You can't bring him here.

That was nearly six months ago. My father hasn't worked since, due to the breakdown. Faye parks that at my curb. And get this: she tells everyone he's depressed because he has cancer and not to speak about it in front of him but people know better. He doesn't have cancer. He's in the choir, teaches Bible class, sits on the ecumenical board – the whole shebang; it would shame him to confess that he can't accept Joe. When a colored family joined the church a couple years ago, he was a regular Welcome Wagon, urging everyone to be tolerant. I hate that word. Church people are the least like Jesus you can imagine.

What should I call what I'm writing – a journal, a testament? You will have searched the apartment and eventually found it in the cedar chest I got for my seventeenth birthday (my hopeless chest, I call it). I embroidered six sets of pillowcases and hemmed a stack of tea towels before losing interest in filling it. As you've discovered, I keep sweaters in it now. The orangey-brown accordion folder holds Joe's letters from Vietnam, organized by month; he may want them back. When I picture someone digging through my stuff, I get goose bumps, as if I've buried a time capsule. Makes me want to tell the whole truth, as they say, to be sure I don't mislead anyone.

For instance, I'm technically not a teller (they get paid more), but nobody else does what I do, either. I'm in charge of vacation and Christmas clubs, U.S. Savings Bonds, and the safety deposit boxes in the vault. I like the variety. I got the job when they put in air conditioning and a woman who'd been there for fifteen years couldn't take the cold, even with a sweater. When it's not busy, I get to calculate the interest on the regular savings accounts and write the amounts on yellow cards. This is not what I thought my career would be. I wanted to be a lawyer, an aspiration my father said was unrealistic. He would have paid for college if I agreed to become a teacher, which – no offense if that's what you are – I found too ordinary. Before I married Joe, I was saving for law school. That money's gone.

Here's something else: I'm not always sorry when Brother D comes over. He keeps Joe from the crying that freaks me out, gets Joe laughing, mostly about stuff they did in 'Nam that I don't find funny, like dropping their pants to show some scared Vietnamese kids that Negroes don't have tails or painting "four more kill-ing days to Christmas" on a Quonset. Their laughing sounds so twisted at times you'd think they were being tortured. But, any kind of laugh from Joe frees me up. When he's depressed, I can't get anything done and my shoulders ache from carrying his mood around with me. With Brother D there, I can do stuff like clean out the refrigerator, change the wax paper lining in the kitchen cabinets, and straighten up the drawers. It's me, not Joe, people will say was the bad housekeeper when they poke around.

I'm not afraid to die, even a little eager in a weird sort of way, assuming something comes after. Once when Joe was choking me I glimpsed how it would be. It felt safe, like being rocked to sleep in someone's arms or maybe going on a space walk. Since then, I'm okay about it, except for not knowing what my body will do. I heard that when you put a dog down its muscles relax, if you know what I mean. I will be so embarrassed if that's true for people. Lately, I've been giving myself an enema before bed. If that doesn't work, please tell whoever had to clean up after me I'm sorry.

Joe was a year ahead of me in school, but I knew him, everybody did; he made most of the touchdowns. We caught the same bus to school, at different stops. He'd be up front in his varsity jacket when I got on – such a charge having a star on my bus. I'd say hi and sit close if I could. He'd say hi, too, but hardly ever look me in the eyes.

Afraid to, he said the night we first hooked up. His old man would have slapped him upside the head – Joe's words – after telling him umpteen times: find yourself next to a white girl, nothing to do but pretend she doesn't exist. Joe's folks grew up in Alabama, you have to make allowances. They feel betrayed, for years having taken Joe to potluck dinners at AME churches all over the state so he'd meet someone safe. He's welcome to go around and see them and his brothers and sister if he doesn't bring me, but only if it's dark outside and he calls ahead.

On the bus, I didn't look at Joe's face, either, for more than was necessary, something I learned before kindergarten when the only dark people I saw were on the way downtown to the doctor's, the bank, and the store that x-rayed my feet before I got new shoes. Faye would pull me to town in a wagon once a week in good weather. Don't stare, she'd say and twist my nose when I did, making my eyes water. I envied those children in the summer, their mini-park with a fountain that sprayed into a wide, oval cement basin. I couldn't play in it because of polio, Faye said, and the notion got buried in me for years that colored people were infectious.

On the bus, even when I spoke to him, I focused on Joe's wide hands, so patient-looking resting on his thighs, the fingers spread open. I wondered whether he was more or less like me inside, whether he hated or envied me. He was different from the cocky ones who strutted down the halls; he kept some of himself back. It upset me that no one else on the bus talked to him. I felt responsible for him, worried when I missed a day.

I was the one who didn't talk to them, he told me not long ago. They asked stupid questions like, we gonna win the game this Saturday, Joe? How the hell would I know?

The year Joe graduated I bought a yearbook and had him autograph it on the bus. To one of the nicest girls in school, he wrote across his picture, God bless. What a letdown. To be honest, I expected more appreciation.

A car backfired last night on the street outside our bedroom and before my brain could identify the sound, Joe rolled me onto the floor and pulled the mattress on top of us, knocking over a lamp we'll have to replace now. Don't move, he whispered.

What's up? I said, winded and startled to find myself on the floor but also – I know this sounds stupid – thrilled he wanted to save me, too.

The enemy's all around, Joe said, but you can't see them.

Wake up, babe, I said, you're here, you're home, and he said, I know where I am. I can look at here and there at the same time.

It's hard to know when Joe's sleep-talking because he doesn't mumble and gets annoyed if I tell him he's dreaming, so I play along or say something else until he wakes.

A car backfired, I said. Could have been a gun, I suppose, but I heard a loud muffler right after, probably some hoods cruising town.

He groaned and stood like a shot, throwing back the mattress. I helped him put the room back together and sat on the end of the bed with him. What a candy-ass I am, he said, scared shitless by a car. I kissed his hands and he said, my poor angel with the violet eyes, not right, you having to put up with this. I walked to the window, raised the shade to let in the moon. I hate it when he talks this way, don't know how to convince him I'm where I want to be.

Only a year not knowing if each day was my last, he said, more to himself than to me. No freedom bird to the States for the VC. Thought more than once about shooting myself in the foot to be lifted out of there. Charlie's got more guts than me.

If you'd grown up there, I said, you'd be used to it, too. Sometimes having no choice only looks like guts.

No, Joe said, they believe in something keeps them firing when they're getting wiped out, when only one left, no way he's gonna survive. Whole time there I never believed like that. I would have died for Darnell, sure, for the others, too, but only because we were connected; nothing to do with belief. Sometimes I'm so lonely for those guys, feels like my chest will explode. Nobody willing to die for you here.

The way he said that made me feel small. Maybe nobody rushing to fall on a grenade, I said, but you and me, we gave up our old lives for each other. I crawled onto the bed behind him and stretched out my spine.

Married people are supposed to do that, he said, it's not the same kind of sacrifice. Know what's different about Darnell since he got back? He's intense as a guerrilla, on a mission, nothing more important than what he's doing.

I lifted my leg and let the moonlight paint a line down the middle of it, making one half light, the other dark, listening to Joe but thinking how hard it would be to hold hands with Brother D and lose consciousness of his color, it's what he wants you to see the most.

Going to school is important, I said.

Sure, sure, Joe said, but Darnell comes out of those meetings buzzing with life. I'm dragging my ass around every day just trying to concentrate, can't keep a thought in my head.

There are people who can help with that, I said. We'll find the money.

No docs, no shrinks, I've told you, Joe said. Darnell doesn't need a shrink. Time I went to those meetings with him, see what that's about.

Black Power, I said, that's what it's about, romantic hooey to get you to sacrifice yourself for your so-called race. It won't get rid of your nightmares.

You don't know that, he said. Darnell says a lot of healing goes on in those meetings. Says only way our people can be sane is accept we're aliens in a foreign land.

My land? While Joe slept, I conjured up the rape of that slave girl so long ago, wondered if she was repulsed by her baby's green eyes, the red in its hair, if she had to close her eyes to nurse it. I wept for a while then got furious at Brother D for telling stories that keep the hate alive. How can you heal when you trade one enemy for another?

The days get shorter and colder and the strangest things make me weepy. My hormones must be out of whack. When the Wurm sisters strolled into the bank this morning, in their matching tweed coats and lace-up shoes, I was overwhelmed with affection for them. I'm ashamed to say I've made fun of them before with Earl, the way they show up once a month to clip bond coupons, their vacant smiles as I unlock the brass gates to the vault, how I carry their heavy box – the biggest size we have – to a closet, show them in, go back to my station and silently count. Before I get to ten, one of them comes out and asks, may we have a scissor, dear? Earl agrees that giving them the scissors right away would spoil it for them. The whole ritual and their saying, scissor, not scissors, usually cracks me up. This morning my eyes filled and whichever one it was had come out for the scissors said, anything wrong, dear? I was thinking how much I'd miss them, isn't that something?

I don't believe in Faye's Hell but there has to be a settling of accounts, so to speak, like balancing out at the bank. Some days I come up short but it's usually just a few bucks and Earl dismisses it with a wave of his hand, no big deal. If I'm a bit short when I get to Heaven or wherever, I hope it's like that.

I've been writing for months not knowing who you'll be. The police officer who makes the official report? Reverend Moore from the church that's no longer mine? God, what if it's Faye and she destroys what I write?

I could use some Valium, it's hard to stay perky, but darned if I'll ask Dr. Eversoll. He makes me call every month to renew my prescription for the Pill, must think delivering me twenty years ago gives him the right. Thought any more about counseling? he asks each time. Who does he think will pay? It frosts me that he assumes I have to be bonkers to love Joe. Frosts me even more that the Pentagon insists Vietnam vets are in such fine shape they require no special treatment. The Pentagon should try sleeping with Joe. And get this: the woman I got at the VA today called them Vietnamese vets, even after I corrected her.

I lost track of Joe once he graduated until December two years ago, less than three months before he landed in Vietnam with the first of the Marines. He's proud of enlisting, proud of making up for his father getting himself 4F to escape the second war to, ha ha, end all wars.

We ran into each other at the Second Presbyterian where my father and Joe's sister were performing Handel's Messiah with every Protestant choir in town, such a huge sound it gave me chills. I wore my white wool coat with the imitation leopard skin collar and matching hat; he was in dress blues two pews in front of me and zap! – spotting him was like stepping onto the bus in high school again, pretending he'd shown up just for me. I studied the back of his head all through the music, mentally tracing the rigid collar around his strong neck. How fitting, I thought, that he'd gone into the service, remembering him on the bus as stoic, brave even. Afterward, I waited for him at the back of the church.

You must like uniforms, I said and he smiled, recognition coming into his eyes.

You must like jungle cats, he said, tapping my hat, such confidence from him giving my stomach a jolt of nervous surprise. He offered me a ride. I ran back to tell my father who was changing out of his choir robe that I was leaving with a friend. I just didn't say which one. Faye wasn't there to dodge, the Messiah always a few choruses too long for her liking.

Where to? Joe said and opened the passenger door, which may seem like a small thing to mention but it's amazing how many guys don't. I was impressed. Said I wouldn't mind going somewhere to talk for a while, to catch up.

We went to a root beer stand that was closed for the winter and sat in the lot until Joe got worried the cops would show up and hassle him for bothering me, so we drove to a park where families skate on the pond and the police ignore couples in cars.

Something inside was telling me to resist Joe, to tell him to take me home, but there with the engine on and the heater full blast, I found myself wondering what he'd taste like, of all things, wondering how big he was and if it would hurt. I'd just broken up with a guy I'd come dangerously close to going all the way with, so I was primed, if you know what I mean, not that it's any excuse. Hard to believe how unresisting I was, you'd think I'd had a Tom Collins. I'm still embarrassed about it.

Joe got into a state when he realized it was my first time. Jesus, what have I done? he said, and I felt guilty like I'd deceived him in some way, but he hadn't asked.

We didn't talk on the drive home except for me to give him directions. He pulled over to drop me off half a block from my house and said, gotta be back at base next week, can I write you? The tenderness in his voice felt like pity and my arms and legs went spongy with shame. No need, I said.

I want to, he said, and when my shoulders shook, he slid over and held me until I was still. I'm so grateful, he said, so undeserving. I would have dissolved into dust if he'd said he was sorry. I said he could write me in care of the bank, I trusted the mail boy. His letter from Camp Lejeune came a few weeks later but I didn't answer, not convinced he wasn't simply feeling obligated. He wrote a second time, about his orders for Vietnam, and I decided it would be unpatriotic not to write back.

I liked having Joe as my secret, exploring the mystery of him without anyone knowing and warning me not to. I wrote question after question, amazed at each piece of himself he revealed, the intelligence and promise of him. I shared my vision of a color-unconscious world and he said they were trying it over there, a rainbow of guys eating out of the same pan. If we can believe in that world together, I wrote, we'll be invincible. The closer he got to leaving, the more he worried about dying. How cruel it would be, he wrote, if one night was all we ever had. I said we can have every night from now on as far as I'm concerned and he wrote back, okay. You may wonder why I don't sleep on the couch; those letters keep me next to him listening for the signs. I'm getting better at rolling off the bed in time.

Been a month since he started the meetings in Newark, three nights a week. I wanted to go with him, but he says he can't bring me there. Someone gave him a white shirt, black pants, and black tie to wear to meetings. You've turned in one uniform for another, I said, and he answered like a robot: it's essential to the demonstration of self-respect.

Nights he's gone, I distract myself with housework. Sometimes I go to the library and read magazines. The latest issue of *Ebony* says that, at one time, it was an insult to call someone black, but now it's in; colored and Negro are out.

Darnell – I've agreed to call him that for Joe's sake – brought a can of Folgers over last night; he can afford to be gracious now that he's won. He brought it into the kitchen where I was clipping recipes from a magazine a customer left behind at the bank.

Hmm, mountain grown, the richest kind, I said like the commercial, but he looked confused so I said, thanks, Joe's at school.

I know, he said and sat across from me, leaning into the table as though he had a confidence to share. I came to talk with you.

Oh, yeah, what about?

You living here, away from your own people. Must be hard.

My, my, you actually care? I felt bad for a second when a ripple crossed his shiny, high forehead as though he were hurt.

He stroked his chin and said, more like appreciate. Your letters got my brother Joseph through some ugly times. He was proud, a white chick writing him every day, didn't know better then, thought he needed you to raise him up. Must make him sad, you here by yourself so much, looking like the loneliest woman on earth.

Darnell likes to play the shrink, to pretend he knows you better than you know yourself. I don't mind spending time with myself, I told him. It's not the same as lonely. Besides, Joe's my people now.

That's just it, he said. He can't be. You haven't earned him, got no right to share in his past, you know what I mean? Integration is a fraud.

Want your own land, Darnell, I said, a reservation? It's done wonders for the Indians.

You're trying to get my goat, he said, but I won't let you. I came over to make peace, to tell you to quit your exile, stop punishing yourself, it won't pay the debt.

What's that supposed to mean? I asked, and he said, loving one black man's not enough to stamp Void on everything your people did to mine. Sharing your pay with Brother Joseph, sharing what you stole from us, is not enough. Over three hundred years we worked for nothing, yes-sirring and no-sirring our asses off, you dig? This country got rich on us.

I didn't do the stealing, I said.

Don't matter, he said. You gotta deal with the unfinished business. You wouldn't have your job if we hadn't worked for nothing. Think about that. If you love that man, be humble enough to admit the truth and stop tempting him away from it.

I sat at the kitchen table long after Darnell left, letting his words soak into me, missing, of all things, my old room in my parents' house, thinking that if Joe and I broke up, I'd be alone forever. I couldn't lie and promise until death do us part to someone else.

The wake of a slave ship has broken over my shore.

I was still up last night, reading, when Joe slipped into our room so quietly I didn't realize it until he was standing beside the bed holding a piece of paper out as if it were a present.

I know why I didn't die over there, he said, his voice sounding worn out, older.

I took the paper from him, on it a drawing of a man on his knees, chained hands reaching up as if in prayer, bulging eyes pleading with someone unseen. I had to turn away from the cruelty of the image. This can't be good for you, I said. What goes on at those meetings?

He knelt beside the bed and held up his hands as though his

wrists were bound. All of us men tonight, he said, we got down on our knees and let this man enter us, let ourselves feel his chains. We stayed that way for ten minutes, felt like hours, my neck hurt so bad from looking up, my eyes from not blinking lest I miss a signal from the brother playing the slave master. If I'd been allowed to speak, I wouldn't have had enough air except to whine. I have never been so moved, felt such communion. He shuddered then smiled as if he'd won a prize.

The thought of those people messing with his mind – practicing witchcraft, maybe, persuading him he could be possessed by a drawing – terrified me. I was furious at their irresponsibility. Get up, I said, pulling at Joe's wrists. He yanked them back.

Look at me, he said, tell me what you see.

You're exhausted, I said. Stop whatever this is and come to bed.

Do you see the slave in me, do you see my blackness?

You know I don't, I said. To identify with that drawing is to be filled with shame.

Whose shame?

His, I said, and everyone else who was ever a slave. How could so many people have thought so little of themselves? I shut up then because something I didn't know I believed until that moment wanted to spill out of my mouth: if I'm to blame for what was done hundreds of years ago, they're to blame for letting it happen.

Joe lowered his arms, sat back on his heels and closed his eyes. You think he should have chosen death over slavery?

He could have fought back, I said, maybe he wouldn't have died.

Tears slipped from Joe's closed eyes and into his nostrils. Some fought back, he said, and they were shot or beaten to death, lynched or torn apart by dogs, God save them. Not their blood in me. It's his. I'm proud of that man. Because he chose life, I live, was spared in 'Nam so I could bear witness for him. Can you appreciate what he did for me?

He curled into a ball on the floor and sobbed. I slipped out of bed and covered his body with mine, wiped his face with my nightgown. I can, I can, I said into his ear, not appreciating it at all but frantic to keep him from losing his mind. Am I the only one who can see his wounds?

Forgive the wobbly writing, spaced out on Valium. Finagled sleeping pills, too. Had to book shrink date right there in Eversoll's office, no intention keeping it. Stubbed toe today, maybe yesterday, doesn't matter, pain so far away couldn't be bothered reacting. How's song go, oh me oh my, do I feel high? Not too high to think this through, be sure what I've written not in wrong hands. It's out of hopeless chest now, in envelope with next month's rent. When this note's done, Mrs. Will, I'll put everything in mail to you. Sorry for the burden, you're the only one I can trust.

Window closing on my opportunity. Joe like caged panther, looking for way out of me, wrong history on my skin. Never really had him, probably made us up. Don't know what else to do but let him kill me; only way he'll get help. Everyone will see how much he needs it. You'll testify to that, come to his defense? Wish I'd invited you up for coffee, would you have come? Thanks for taking us in.

Trick is dope myself enough to not struggle, not pull hands off neck. Take too much I ruin the plan. I'm ready, I think, maybe tonight, same dread and excitement as when first gave myself to Joe, a gift, not a sacrifice, please tell him it was that.

Passing Through

All that lives must die / Passing through nature to eternity.
—Gertrude in *Hamlet*

C831

"I'LL QUIT SCHOOL AND TAKE CARE OF YOU," SPENCER SAID INTO the hollowness behind her.

Trudy stood before the Christmas tree in the living room where, only twelve hours before, her brother-in-law, Jack, had staggered across the floor and eased her husband's stiffening body onto the couch. Cradling it as you would a sleeping child.

"We left the tree lights on all night," she said.

"You always said the place would be mine someday. I'm ready now."

She turned sharply and looked into his eyes. Pond blue like his father's, but closer together and lacking the humour. "I haven't died." The property was in her name, had been in her family since 1906 when her great-grandfather homesteaded the land. "I expect you to finish school." Spencer was a semester away from a degree in agricultural and bio-resource engineering. Fancy words for farming, but gone were the days when you could rely on hard work and the *Farmer's Almanac*.

"I don't need a degree to run this place. I already know more than Dad ever did."

"You'll never know that much," she said, sorry when she saw his wounded face. Pictures of him as a child – laughing, acting the clown – hung on the walls. She still could summon the intensity she'd felt for him back then – like falling in love day after day. He'd

97

grown up so serious. His sunny hair had darkened and begun to recede. He looked too old to be her son.

"I can't talk about this now," she said.

The wind up the valley stung her face as she rode out on horseback to the funeral, her head sludgy with sorrow, no hat on the frizzy red hair Dave had likened to a brush fire. The sound of hooves on crusty snow bit the air as Jack rode on one side of her, Spencer on the other. Wearing his father's long, black outback coat and wide-brimmed black hat, Spencer held the reins of the riderless King trotting beside him.

"A bit much, don't you think?" Jack said. His voice was deep and sometimes so muffled you'd think he was talking to himself.

"He wants to honour King," Trudy said. "What's the harm?" Felled by a stroke, Dave had one foot in the Palomino's stirrups when Jack found him along the back fence line.

As far as Jack could tell, King hadn't moved. "Son of a gun looked like he was stuffed," he'd said. "Never stood like that for me." Jack was a farrier, used to horses that pulled and reared, but King confounded him.

The small southern Alberta farming community would miss Dave – never too busy to pitch in at branding and herding time or when fields needed swathing. Nearly two hundred gathered on the frozen earth under a bleak sky, their faces registering the weather as well as the occasion. Those on horseback formed a circle around the ones who stood hugging themselves against the cold. Dave's parents clutched each other as Spencer rode in straight-backed and brave. Trudy spotted colleagues from the branch where she'd been a teller for as long as she and Dave had been married. Twenty-four years of asking: "How do you want that – tens or twenties?"

King snorted, dipped his head, and pawed the snowy ground Dave had been so thrilled to see. He'd hollered for her like a big kid: "It's snowing, Red! Hear the ground sucking it in, the grass already growing?"

Icy word clouds left the United Church minister's mouth. For her in-laws' sake, she'd arranged a traditional service, but not in a joyless church. On the rise, instead, where she and Dave would ride to study Old Chief Mountain's face touching the sky.

Later, bowls and platters materialized in the dining room: a whole ham, fried chicken, baked beans, scalloped potatoes, green beans, coleslaw, biscuits and honey, brownies, and rice pudding. The attention to detail moved her. Someone had thought of paper plates and napkins, someone else, mustard and mayonnaise. As most of the neighbours were Mormons, however, no one had brewed coffee. She made herself an instant and squeezed through the crowd spilling onto the unheated porch.

"Not a sadder time for this to happen," a woman from down the road said. "But look on the bright side. With so many around for the holidays, you got a good turnout."

Trudy was leaning against the side of the house looking at the bright side of the moon when Spencer found her. "You and Dad shouldn't have dumped the sheep," he said, rubbing his arms. He'd come looking for her in shirtsleeves. "They're more adaptable to drought and hard winter. I'm gonna bring them back."

"Oh, sweetheart," she said, opening her coat to him, "give it a rest."

It was two years since Jack showed up back in town, things having gone sour between him and a woman in Red Deer. Around that time, mad cow closed the U.S. border to live cattle and they could no longer afford to hire even the occasional hand. In exchange for labour evenings and weekends, Dave offered Jack the log cabin within eyeshot of their home, the one she'd grown up in – a ranch house with peeling yellow paint.

"He'll have weekdays to get a shoeing business going," Dave said. "It's always bothered me, the cabin standing empty." Mostly, she suspected, because she retreated to it whenever he got too full of himself and talked down to her.

"I can't believe you gave it to him without asking me."

"I hate that cabin," Spencer said, his voice a slap. "When I was little and you'd leave Dad and me to go there, it made me want to run away, too." A picture he drew at school came back to her:

the cabin with angry black crayon streaks over the windows and door. *Not your usual careful work,* the teacher had written.

The cabin was her honeymoon home, a gift from her parents. She and Dave lived in it only a year before a tractor-trailer jack-knifed on an icy road in front of her folks' pick-up. They'd taken over the business, keeping a hundred and fifty ewes and three hundred cows for close to twenty years until drought left much of the pasture scorched and useless. The sheep went first. After mad cow, all but seventy of the cows. Through it all, she kept the cabin like new, chasing spiders and mice away, laundering curtains and linens so they'd stay fresh.

"He's only gonna sleep there, for chrissakes," Dave said.

"He better clean up after himself."

Jack tanned darker than Dave and had eyes and hair the colour of crude – "our changeling," his mother joked. Elbows on the table, he forked his food as if doing you a favour. When the rest of the family debated one thing or another, he'd lean back in his chair, silent and watchful. She caught him staring at her more than once.

After moving into the cabin, he stopped in for breakfast a few times a week at Dave's invitation – early, so Dave could see to the cows and she could get to the bank. One morning, Jack scooped up the plates from the table and filled the sink with soapy water.

"What are you doing?" she said. "Don't you have to hit the road?"

"*Hit the road, Jack,*" he sang, flicking water at her with long, agile fingers. "First appointment isn't 'til ten, a critter partial to foot massages with dishpan hands."

She hadn't seen this side of Jack. She liked a sense of humour in a man.

"Does this filly have a name?"

"What makes you think it's a she? Maybe I swing both ways."

"Ha!" She grabbed a towel to dry the dishes. "Why'd you take up shoeing?"

"It's honest work, important, too. A bad shoer can cripple a horse."

"You must have stories. How come you don't say much?"

"Conversation is an Olympic sport in our family, present company excluded. I'm better one-on-one."

She liked that he noticed she was different. Started listening for his 4x4 coming up the gravel road to their place, watching for him to go in and out the cabin's red door.

Spencer reluctantly returned to the University of Saskatoon the middle of January. Trudy walked him out to his metallic gray Mazda. He'd bought it at sixteen with money she and Dave had set aside for him from the sale of the sheep. The car had been nine years old even then. She worried about it breaking down on some lonely stretch of highway. "Call as soon as you get there. Call if you run into trouble."

"I wish you wouldn't try this alone," he said. "Makes me feel like shit."

"Your uncle's still here. Besides, I worked the ranch in the past and I've always kept the books. I might have a few brain cells left."

He put a hand on her shoulder. Something Dave used to do. "'Course you do. It's just that we're running out of time. Maybe I'm mental, but I've felt Dad around ever since the funeral. I think he chose to die so I could rescue the business."

She didn't know whether to laugh or stomp on his foot. "It's good to have a sense of destiny. Your dad always said you had manure in your veins."

"If only he'd listened, I could have taught him so much."

She did laugh at that, and Spencer's eyes narrowed the way they had when he was a child and got angry. A positively evil look that prompted Dave to joke that she'd given birth to the Devil's Spawn. They knew he'd go off and break something for them to find later, something they cared about. Her grandmother's teapot one time.

"I'm sorry," she said. "It's just that he felt the same way about you."

After Spencer left, she waited on the cabin steps for Jack to get home. A Chinook had blown in that day. The warm, dry air left her longing for the purple and yellow prairie anemones that would decorate the grazing land in a few months. Life would return to normal. She'd wake up to Dave spooning her, his hard-on against her butt.

When she heard Jack's tires on the gravel, she moved to where he always parked the truck. He rolled down his window, releasing a smell of dust and horse barn that washed over her like new grief. "What's up?" he said.

"I was wondering if you might be able to give me some extra hours. 'Til Spencer graduates."

"You gotta think about selling. Dave figured it would take years to come back, if ever. He reckoned you guys were hooped."

His sunglasses reflected her whiny mouth, the sudden anger she felt at Dave. "This ranch survived two world wars, the Depression, more than a few recessions. I can't be the one who loses it. He had a little life insurance, but it won't last. So, will you help me?"

He pushed his cap back and stared at her so hard, she looked down at her boots. "Okay, Lady Blue. It's my slow time, anyway. But you're in charge. I don't want the responsibility."

He came over that night, clean-shaven and with a six-pack of Big Rock. She was taking ornaments off the tree. He popped a can and handed it to her.

"Don't know as I ever told you how nice it was to look over and see that tree in the window," he said. "I took it for granted."

"It went up late again this year because Dave waited for Spencer to get home from school. They always did that together, cutting it down."

Jack made a move for the couch and she waved him off. She hadn't let anyone on it since Christmas Eve. She sat on the floor in front of the coffee table and gestured for him to join her. He lowered himself, groaning as his bones cracked.

"I thought Dave would always be there," he said. "He was dependable, you know? I mean you could depend on him being who he was. True to himself."

"He wasn't moody, that's for sure. Not like Spencer. He refuses to room with anyone at school. I wonder if he has any fun."

"Could be the boy's a little different, but who's to say what's normal? Some folks would probably like to smooth me out like a bump on the road."

They sat for a while in silence, a strange experience for her. Dave had always filled their conversational gaps. Jack handed her another beer.

"Dave was a real shit disturber when he was young," he said. "He ever tell you about when him and me was in the barn fooling around with a pitchfork? He was probably fifteen, me twelve. Pop had a few pigs in those days. Dave threw that fork like a spear and it went right through the boar's ear. Man, were we scared. He pinned that fuckin' boar to the wall. It squealed like a … like a…"

"Stuck pig?" She'd heard the story a million times from Dave.

He laughed and she noticed that one of his teeth was discoloured, as though the nerve had died. "Yeah, just like. Then there was the time a skunk got under the porch and he shot it. The smell went through the whole house. Never seen Mom so pissed off." He went quiet for a moment then ran his fingers through his thick hair, exposing the grey underneath.

"I'm gonna miss him." A tear slipped down his face. "Jesus, look at me."

She reached over to pat his back. The warmth of him shot through her hand and she pulled back. He stood and stumbled toward the bathroom, wiping his face on his sleeve. She opened another beer and looked at the piano her mother had taught her to play. Dead by forty-four, her mother hadn't gone without a husband next to her in the night. Trudy got up, opened the piano bench and pulled out a songbook worn from page turning. Sat and played *If You Were the Only Girl in the World*. Sang in a clear, high voice that amazed her.

Jack came up behind her. "I've never heard you sing."

"Yeah, well, I can be shy." He sat beside her and, in a growly monotone, sang along to *Carolina in the Morning*. She laughed until her eyes ran over and she no longer could see the notes.

It seemed natural, later, to curl up next to him on the bed she'd shared with Dave only a month before in what she still thought of as her parents' room. Jack staying the next few days seemed as it should be, too, a harmless step along the continuum of moving on. They slept back to back. He filled the room with a smell she liked, of freshly dug earth and camping out and working up an appetite.

He reached for her one night when she was breathing him in.

"I always envied him you," he said later. "Think he's watching us?"

"Spencer thinks he chose to die," she said. Chose to leave her.

Jack was more demanding than Dave. "Do me," he said, and she didn't know what he meant. She felt like a hick, a *farmer's wife*, ashamed at her lack of imagination, furious at Dave – so unfair, she knew – for not preparing her for life without him. Sometimes she wanted Jack to go away; it was too much for her. But his expectations excited her, made her feel powerful.

Spencer called one Sunday, his voice tight with energy, to tell her he'd been dreaming about Dave. She didn't want to think about Dave. Or Spencer. She wanted to feel unencumbered, adrift on the river of desire that had broken through her mourning.

"I feel such love in the dreams, I wake up crying."

He'd been dry-eyed at the funeral. Perhaps she'd been wrong to insist he go back to school. She'd gotten over her parents easily enough but, then, she'd had Dave. And so much to do. She honestly didn't miss them right away. Not until Spencer's birth, when she cried like a forsaken child. Look what I made, she wanted to tell them.

"You're grieving," she said. "Perfectly natural."

"I don't think that's it, well maybe a little. Wish I'd thanked him more. Can't believe I argued with him about meaningless shit like grazing techniques."

"Well, there you go," she said and changed the subject.

Jack moved a few things over but continued to park his truck by the cabin. He'd duck out the side door and head for the barn whenever he heard a car coming. "You need your neighbours," he said. "No sense shifting their tongues into gear so soon."

"There'll be no pleasing some, no matter how long we wait," she said. "They expect me to spend the rest of my life getting ready to join Dave." She packed up Dave's clothes for Spencer to look through later. He might disapprove of her and Jack at first, but he'd get over it.

She and Jack worked the ranch together, ending each day shaking off the manure and dirt, showering together. She corralled her hair into a rubber band and tucked it under a cap. Her face got chapped and her muscles tight. She felt more authentic, like an intense beam focused on something at last that mattered. Thinking about returning to the bank made her claustrophobic. She'd kept the job all that time because she earned more than Dave could by hauling silage, the only paying job he ever held. If he had appreciated her letting him have the freedom of all that sky, he never said.

Spencer's midterm break came in February. Jack moved into the cabin for the week so she could slide Spencer into the news. She was in the kitchen when he arrived.

"These don't look like Dad's," his voice said from out of nowhere, making her jump. He'd come through the porch and was holding Jack's skates up by the laces. She forgot they were there, leaning against the freezer next to hers. She'd gone through the house that morning collecting evidence Jack had missed – a shirt in her closet, his razor in the medicine chest. She hadn't thought to look on the porch.

"Jeez," she said, her hand on her chest. "You should feel my heart. I didn't hear you drive up." She took the skates from him and set them on the floor, gave him a quick hug.

"You smell like fries."

"I stopped for a burger along the way." He dropped his backpack to the floor and draped his parka over a kitchen chair. "You look thinner. Is that a new sweater?"

She was in tight black jeans and a turquoise sweater Jack said made her green eyes pop like a wildcat's. She'd forgotten Spencer was used to seeing her in shapeless sweats. She felt almost naked.

"Just a cheap thing I got at Zeller's."

"It feels brighter in here," he said. "You change the lights?"

"No, the walls. Jack painted them last weekend. Lemon Meringue. You like?"

"He has time to paint?"

"We're keeping up with the chores real well. You look beat. How was the drive?"

"Roads were clear. I made good time. Whose skates are those?"

She looked down at them, frowning slightly, as though struggling to remember. "Jack's, maybe? Yes, of course. We went skating one day." Her words raced out like startled mice. "Such a clean freeze on the pond this year, no ripples."

There was always a splash of re-entry when Spencer came home from school, some awkwardness as they bridged the distance that had grown between them. It was greater this time, her distance entirely, making her nervous. She took a breath and spoke more deliberately. "Now, tell me about those circles under your eyes."

He straddled a chair. "I can't get back to sleep after I dream about Dad. Too wired, too excited about what it means. Some nights he's on King, wearing those dorky shades, grinning as if he's sold a cow for a thousand bucks. Other times he's at the end of a long hallway in front of a gigantic computer, his fingers flying over the keyboard. I've never had dreams so real. Does he visit you?"

She didn't want to tell him she'd been jolted out of sleep one night by Dave's voice calling her, that she'd tiptoed through the house afterwards with a flashlight and a feeling of dread. "I hardly ever remember my dreams," she said.

She turned back to the counter, to the file she'd been searching through when he arrived. "I'm looking for that recipe you like – the one with the hard-boiled eggs and pickles inside. Was it Meatloaf Surprise?"

"I'll take this stuff to my room," he said, picking up his backpack, disappointment in his voice. She let out the breath she didn't know she'd been holding. She was disappointed, too. He expected her to help him keep Dave alive.

Later that night, as Spencer slept down the hall, she called Jack's cell phone and, keeping her voice low, said, "I couldn't do it. I need your help."

"You want *me* to break it to him?"

"No, no. Just spend some time with him before I tell him."

"What for?"

"He's always wanted you to care about him. Mooned over you when he was little. Remember him asking you to play Hot Wheels all the time?"

"No. But I was a selfish prick then. Still am, I reckon."

"He misses his father. I think he'll accept us better if he's closer to you."

"Listen, I don't know where you and me are going, but you can't put your life back the way it was. I'm no Dave. Never wanted children, for one thing. Don't see why people have 'em."

For a second chance, she thought. You hope they'll be a better version of you. She had failed her parents in that, managing to keep only a fraction of their livestock. Spencer was better educated, but she wondered if he could stand on his own. Wondered if she and Dave had made life a little too easy for him.

"I didn't realize how hard it would be to face him," she said. "Maybe we should wait until he graduates. 'Til he's over Dave a little more."

"Sure. It's your call. We don't have to do it ever. Say the word, I'm outta here."

It was tempting. She was exhausted. It had been so easy with Dave, so unchallenging. She thought about spending her days and nights with Spencer. The widow and her son, watching *Wheel of Fortune* every evening after putting the cows to bed.

"I don't want you to leave."

Early the next morning, she watched from the picture window as Spencer strolled out to the cows. They were lying around the feed

bin like a heap of discarded carpets. Jack was there already, toss-
ing them hay. Spencer got a pitchfork and started to help. Such a
small thing, but it lifted her enough to envision the three of them
in days to come banding together to keep the homestead. She and
Spencer would work the ranch. Jack would go back to shoeing
full-time, bringing in the cash they needed. Spencer could have the
cabin to himself. He liked being alone.

A few hours later, she saw them by the barn working on a pump.
When she checked again around noon, they were gone. She was
along the east side of the house dumping coffee grounds into the
composter when they stepped out of the cabin and raced each
other to her side, laughing loudly, red in the face.

"We might've had a beer or two," Jack said to her questioning
look.

"I told Uncle Jack about my plans for the place," Spencer said.
"He's going to loan me some money to get the sheep started."

"Really," she said. She bit her lower lip and squinted at Jack.

"The boy's got some great ideas," Jack said. "First off, get rid of
the cows. Then, plant canola to sell for cash. Other stuff – solar
energy, new irrigation techniques."

"Sometimes I feel like a furnace ready to blow with all the ideas
burning inside me," Spencer said. He took off his gloves and pulled
a paper from his parka. "We roughed out the numbers. It'll take a
while to break even, but we should get by with what you earn at
the bank. Won't need much help from the neighbours. Sheep are
a heck of a lot easier than cows."

"We're gonna be shepherds," Jack said, opening his arms wide.
"How 'bout that? Gonna get us a couple of staffs – what's the
plural of staff, staves? Gonna get us a couple of staves and several
coats of many colours."

Spencer put his hands together as if in prayer. "Be not afraid, the
angel said. I bring you news of great joy." He looked light-hearted
enough to float away. She wanted to be happy for him but a cavity
had opened in her chest.

"You can be the Virgin Mary," Jack said. He laughed so hard
he snorted, sending Spencer into fits.

"I hate to piss in your puddle, boys, but I'm not going back to the bank."

"Did they fire you?" Spencer asked, his smile disintegrating.

"No. I'm not going back, that's all."

"We can't make it without outside income, Mom."

"You better get a job then." She turned abruptly and headed back to the house.

Jack hurried after her. "Hey, what gives? Why are you p.o.'d?"

"You can't push me aside like that. And how come you've got money to burn all of a sudden?" She opened the porch door and let it fly back in his face. Threw her jacket and gloves on the freezer. She was so livid she didn't know where to go, settled on the kitchen, Jack right behind her.

"C'mon," he said, pulling her into an embrace. "Cut me some slack. I was trying to help like you asked. Bonding with the boy."

They hadn't noticed Spencer following them in.

"Were you two getting it on when Dad was alive?"

"Shit," Trudy said softly. She sank to the floor, her back against the cupboards. Spencer stood in the doorway, his arms dangling, his face a question mark.

"I was waiting for the right time to tell you," she said. "Jack and I are making a home together." They had agreed on those words, thought they'd come across as responsible and reassuring. With the proper set-up.

"Nothing went on when your dad was here," Jack said. "I swear." He held his hands out, palms up. Trudy was embarrassed for him.

"It just happened," she said. "We were so sad by ourselves, then sad together."

Spencer put his fist to his mouth and blew softly on it. "That's cool," he said. "You were sad. I can relate." He turned and left the room.

Trudy thumped the back of her head against the cupboard, one, two, three times.

"Hey, hey," Jack said. He dropped to the floor beside her and took her hand. They sat like that until Spencer returned with his backpack.

"I'd like to stay in the cabin tonight." He looked at Jack. "If you don't mind sleeping here."

Jack looked at her.

"Fine," she said. As though her opinion mattered.

"Give me a few minutes," Jack said. "I'll clear out my stuff."

After he left, Trudy pulled herself up and followed Spencer onto the porch. It smelled of wet boots and a pine funeral wreath that lay forgotten on the floor. The cold went right through her. She retrieved her jacket from the top of the freezer.

"Nothing is forever, sweetheart," she said.

Spencer punched the wall with his fist. "It was supposed to be my time."

"What do you mean?"

"You were supposed to believe in *me*. Everything's shit now." He kicked the door open and walked out into the dying light.

She spent a fitful evening replaying Spencer's words, stung by his inability to see how much she *had* believed in him. Working at a job she hated, selling off livestock so there'd be a piece of land for him to inherit. She slept, eventually, until Jack shook her roughly and shouted, "Get up! Cabin's on fire."

She heard popping; saw shadows spiking on the bedroom wall. The bedside clock read 3:10 a.m.

"I'll wake Spencer," she said. Then she remembered where he was.

She grabbed her robe and stepped into loafers. Bolted through the living room and out the porch. Jack was paces ahead, carrying a shovel.

"Spencer!" she yelled. Running across the field towards a stack of smoke twisting like a tornado, she breathed through his failing lungs, saw through his stinging eyes. The fire consumed the cabin as though it had started in all places at once. It generated so much heat and light it might have been a day in Hell.

"Did you call 911?" she shouted. Jack tossed snow onto the fire. Hopeless.

"What for? There's no hydrant."

"Jesus, Jack! Not for the fire. For Spencer."

No time to run back and phone. She pulled her robe up to cover her mouth and looked at what faced her. A wall of yellow and orange flames, beautiful in a way, compelling. She imagined her mind, not the fire, illuminating the scene, leaving all around it in darkness. Imagined being swallowed up by the burning light. It felt mystical and right. If there was a God, he'd accept her in place of Spencer. She stepped closer and closer, testing the heat and her resolve.

"Trudy, wait!" Jack shouted, sprinting toward her and pointing. Spencer was coming around the corner of the cabin, taking long, purposeful strides. A taller, leaner version of Dave in parka and jeans. A miracle.

She ran to him, fell on her knees and clutched his legs. If she'd been forced to choose between Jack and Spencer at that moment, the decision would have been easy. She turned her head to the side to wipe her tears on his pants. Saw the gas can hanging from his hand and looked up. "You did this?"

His back was to the fire. She couldn't see his face. "You need the occasional purging fire," he said. "Textbook farming." He dropped the can at her side, walked to his car and drove off.

She watched the Mazda turn into a speck on the main road, listened to the thrumming in her ears then got up off her knees.

Jack came up beside her. "Want me to go after him?"

She shook her head and turned back to the fire. Bits of ruffled curtain fluttered out of a shattered window, childish dollhouse curtains. Her mother had sewn them from blue and white Delft-patterned cotton as a wedding surprise.

"I never wanted that cabin," she said. "I wanted to live in an apartment above the hardware store, but Dad wouldn't hear of it. It hurt that he didn't trust me to know what I wanted."

Neighbours started arriving at dawn. She escaped into the house, leaving Jack to make excuses for her. They'd believe she was too upset to talk even though she wasn't. She was weary enough to sleep for days, but calm and even hopeful. She and Spencer had been growing apart for years. As painful as their confrontation had been, she saw it as a way for them to start over. A purging, as Spencer had said. She shouldn't have left him so much to Dave, should have seen that, like her, he needed a lot of rope.

The county fire department inspector came out around noon. The blaze had been seen for kilometres. As they stood outside the charred cabin, Jack told the inspector he'd left the wood stove untended and flammable supplies nearby. She hadn't asked him to lie, but she didn't contradict him. No sense making it even harder for Spencer to come back. The cabin wasn't insured. No one could accuse them of fraud.

She called the university to be sure Spencer had returned. Tried his cell phone and the residence several times a day but he hung up when he heard her voice. She made the seven-hour drive to Saskatoon, but he refused to see her. Jack urged her to sell, but she insisted Spencer would come around eventually. He just had to. He was too much like her to let go so easily. Too drawn to possibilities, to the redemption of spring.

She still hadn't heard from him when the first calf arrived, hip-locked and dead. They needed the tractor to pull it out of the mother.

Cocktails with Charles

Love sought is good, but given unsought is better.
—Olivia to Viola in *Twelfth Night*

❦

IT WASN'T EXACTLY THE WALDORF-ASTORIA. PERVERTS WOULD steal your underwear if you didn't stay through all the cycles. But the laundry room was bereft of a chair, so Mira sat barefoot and crossed-legged on the sorting table on a sweltering August day in 1975, wearing only the lightest of halter tops and her brother's swim trunks. The smell of fabric softener cloyed the air. Sweat pooled between her breasts and turned her short, black hair into frizzy ringlets.

The door opened with a kick. A pixie of a woman glided across the linoleum floor, toes out like a ballerina, carrying a yellow plastic basket. Mira was just as short, but this woman couldn't have weighed more than a hundred pounds. She looked lost inside a lavender shift that fell from puny shoulders to ankles Mira could easily have gotten a hand around. Her wispy hair was the colour of pumpkin pie.

"Holy Toledo," the pixie said in a surprisingly grown-up voice. "You'd think they could spring for a fan." She set the basket on the floor, pulled out a towel, and propped the door open with it.

"You mean this isn't the sauna?"

"Oh, you're gonna be fun." The pixie's smile dove clear down into Mira's forlorn heart. "I'm Angel Alfredsson from 103."

"Mira Hakala, 422. I've been in for three weeks. The judge gave me life."

Angel's laugh made Mira think improbably of sleigh bells and deep, cool snow.

"It *is* like a cell in here," Angel said. "A window would've been nice."

"Don't mind me," Mira said, aware of a sudden lifting of her mood. "It's just that I left a doorman, exercise room, and pool in Edina."

"Ah. Did you see that Guindon cartoon in the paper?" Angel said, stuffing a washing machine. "The one where the woman says: 'You don't *move* to Edina, you *achieve* Edina.'"

"No, I didn't." Shit. She'd come across as a snob. The buzzer on the dryer went off. Her thighs made a sucking sound as she slid off the table.

"Dippity darned," Angel said, studying a sock. "My big guy must go looking for mud."

"Your husband?" Mira opened the dryer and groaned. She'd left a Kleenex in a pocket.

"No, no, no, my number one son Anthony. He's nine. Matthew is six." Angel held up a small Minnesota Twins jersey. "They're huge fans."

"Me, too, even if the team is limping right now. You alone with the kids?" Mira snuck her brother's underwear into a duffel bag. Tissue snowed onto the floor. She looked around for a broom or a dustpan.

"Alas, I am. You?"

"Just my echo, my shadow, and me."

"Brenda Lee. Or was it the Ink Spots? My mother loved the Ink Spots."

Mira's mother had been almost certifiable over the Harmonicats, made them take "mouth organ" lessons. As if she and Marko weren't weird enough. "Does your mother live close?" Mira hand-swept the tissue bits and put them in the garbage can. The room had one of those, at least.

"Possibly. She's in the Mid-Causal Plane, I think. She and my dad. They disengaged together, five years ago on New Year's Eve."

Mira had no idea what Angel was talking about, but it was fun.

"My parents are in matching urns in a box I haven't unpacked yet," she said, getting into the spirit. "They're more an accent than the main decorating event."

Angel pressed her fingers against her eyes.

"You okay?" Mira asked.

"Yes. Just trying to see you with my inner eyes. Trying to get past that crooked smile you're hiding behind."

A nut case. A beautiful, nervy nut case. Mira stuffed the rest of her clothes unfolded into her bag and said, "See ya."

Back in her apartment she dropped the bag on the floor and smiled into the hall closet mirror. Definitely crooked. Marko's wasn't. She'd gotten so used to looking into his face and seeing her own, she often missed the less than obvious differences between them. She padded to the living room and stood crucifix-style in front of the whining air conditioner. Tried to picture Angel stopping by for a beer. She'd be swallowed up by the black leather couch and loveseat, the humongous glass and chrome tables. Marko had chosen them. From conception until four months ago, they had never lived apart, refused to sleep in separate rooms until they were fifteen. M&M, they called themselves. She was the peanut one: hard on the outside *and* the inside, with only a thin layer for anyone to get in. Anyone else, that is. For twenty-eight years, Marko had always been there.

She found the box she was looking for in the stack against the living room wall, dug through the bubble wrap and pulled out three urns. She couldn't have told Angel about Marko after the bit about their parents. It would have made her seem pathetic.

She took a shower, slipped on a pair of Marko's jockeys and got into his bed. Hers was the one she had dumped in the move. She curled up facing the clock radio and took the cool of the sheets into her skin. It wasn't even eight, but she didn't know what to do with herself in the evenings anymore.

It had been Marko's idea to get the red and black Boss 351 Mustang. It looked all wrong in the parking lot of the new place, Mira realized later that week, when Angel pulled up beside her in a rusting Pontiac with an ailing muffler. Mira slunk down in her seat but – what was she thinking? – it was a convertible. Angel stepped from her car and looked over, shading her eyes from the last of the sun. The buttons on her yellow blouse lay perfectly straight on her boyish chest. At fifteen, Mira had tried starving herself to look like that, trying to look like Marko, actually. She stopped when her parents said she'd end up in a psycho ward and never see him again.

"You just getting home from work, too?" Angel asked. Mira gave her a little wave and climbed out of the Mustang. Angel looked even more fragile in the open air. How could babies have travelled through those tiny hips?

Angel opened the door to the back seat where two boys, book-ended by assorted boxes, were fighting over a rubber arm. The bigger one looked out at Mira with Marko's – and her own – heavy-lidded eyes. Her legs went spongy.

Angel grabbed the arm as the boys tumbled out. "Quieten down, now," she told them to no effect.

They headed for a dusty piece of playground.

Angel turned to Mira. "I demonstrate venipuncture and injections, among other things. I'd still be nursing if I could get decent shifts but, alas, I'm stuck peddling medical supplies. My trunk and back seat overfloweth."

Angel couldn't be seriously mental if someone trusted her with needles. "I'm in sales, too," Mira said.

"I just *knew* you were a kindred spirit. What do you sell?"

"Time and image," Mira said, parroting the instructor of the course she had passed to move out of Typing. Then, feeling like an idiot for trying to impress Angel, she said, "Advertising. On The Good Neighbor station. A new job for me."

"Time and image," Angel said, almost reverently. A tiny gold stud in her earlobe flashed in the sun like a beacon. "Rhonda would love that." Angel explained that Rhonda was a spiritual guide, no longer stuck in the physical world. "She comes through a woman named Jackie."

"Like a radio signal?"

"Sort of. She uses Jackie's vocal chords. Only men came through the channellers I tried before. So, I said to myself, women can't speak after they disengage? Too busy sweeping up cosmic dust?"

Mira laughed and Angel's little bow-shaped mouth laughed back. She pulled a card from her purse and handed it to Mira. *Unleash Your Creative Powers with Rhonda.* "Study group every Tuesday night. Ten dollars. Want to go with me next week?"

Ten bucks for an evening with Angel. "Sure," Mira said.

They took Angel's car. It smelled of mildew and Angel's princess-sweet cologne. Mira stuck her hand out the window and pushed against the wind. The August heat and noisy muffler brought back the summer after high-school graduation when her parents took a rowboat out on a lake and drowned. A rowboat, for God's sake. How embarrassing was that? After the funeral, Marko put bricks in the trunk of their father's Galaxie for a cool, low look and gave the exhaust a monster death rattle. They drove around the city, radio blasting, laughing and crying and holding hands.

"Minneapolis has the world's worst weather," Angel said.

"Yeah," Mira said, "just when you think hell couldn't be any hotter, hell freezes over."

"Ha! You're good for me, Lady. I need to laugh. I created the most awful day for myself. Late for two appointments, late collecting the boys. Anthony was cross with me. Matty was starving; he's always starving. I had dinner on their plates in a record six minutes. Carrot sticks, instant mashed potatoes, and minute steak – which takes longer than a minute to cook, incidentally, just like it takes almost two minutes to play the 'Minute Waltz.' Anyway, it still wasn't fast enough. I should be home with them. Rhonda would say: 'Why create the need for guilt?'" Angel's slender fingers measured an inch of air. "I'm this close to marrying Charles."

Mira felt a surprising stab of disappointment but made the obligatory inquiry.

"I've known him since I was eight. My first piano teacher. He was one of the family when my parents were alive, over at our house every holiday, every Sunday afternoon. My mother felt sorry for him. We've talked about marriage off and on, but just in fun, or at least I thought so. For goodness sake, we've never even kissed, except on the cheek. Then last week, out of the blue, he asked me to seriously consider it."

"He was teaching piano when you were eight? He must be a lot older than you."

"Twenty years this time. Irrelevant, really, considering how many lives we've had together."

"Come again?"

"I shouldn't say *had*. According to Rhonda, there's no past, present, or future. That means Charles and I are living this wild, simultaneous existence in ancient Cathay, Mayan Mexico, fifth-century Ireland, the Alps in six hundred something, Elizabethan England, Australia in the twenty-second century, a planet our telescopes can't see, and here, of course."

Mira wanted to laugh but Angel sounded convinced. "How do you know all this?"

"From study group and a woman who does past life regression. I stopped going after she brought me out of hypnosis by saying," – she dropped her voice an octave – "'you are back in the twentieth century where you are a *very* attractive woman.' Why did she have to say that?"

Mira had never met anyone who actually believed in that stuff. It was a pick-up line in a bar – *Say, didn't I know you in a past life?* "Maybe she didn't want to leave you stranded as Quasimodo," she said. "Were you ever Quasimodo?"

"I doubt it. Only a few of my lives are as men. Rhonda says I need to release more of my animus so I can coach my sons into manhood. If I marry Charles, I won't have to worry about that. How about you? Anyone special in your life?"

"No." Marko had fixed her up with different guys from time to time but they always turned out to be horny creeps. She'd know when the right one came along, he said, but the right one never came along for him, either.

Jackie's apartment was on the second floor of a building along a dodgy section of Lake Street. If this was a scam, she wasn't spending her riches on lavish digs. Two men on the dark side of fifty – one with a grey ponytail – and a woman who shouldn't have been wearing a sleeveless dress were already there, looking chummy on a long brown tweed couch. They stood to hug Angel. She and Mira took worn out mustard-coloured armchairs opposite the couch. Jackie sat across the room in a La-Z-Boy, smiling like a Tupperware party hostess. Angel handed her ten bucks to a man behind a small table fiddling with a tape recorder and Mira did the same. Two tall oscillating fans made a rhythmic buzz as they shoved hot air around.

"It's time," Jackie said. "Would our newcomer like to say a few words?"

Mira declined. She didn't want to tip off any so-called spirit. Wanted to see what it came up with on its own.

After Jackie reminded them she'd be slipping into a trance, she closed her eyes. Nothing happened for several minutes. Mira kept her eyes on Angel who sat on the edge of her chair like a hopeful child. Finally, a different voice arrived – through Jackie's nose, it sounded like.

"Everybody comfy, everybody's *tukhes* on a soft seat?"

"Yes, Rhonda," the regulars said in unison.

"Good. May you have only things to smile about this evening. Who's first?"

"If I may?" Angel said.

"Certainly."

"I've been asked to seriously consider a marriage proposal," Angel said. The woman in the sleeveless dress gave a little whoop. Mira slid down in her chair.

"Hu ha," Rhonda said. "Who's asking? Name and location, please."

"You know who it is."

"Humour me."

"Charles Stammler. Capitola, California."

A long pause followed. Mira wondered if Jackie had fallen asleep.

"Aha, okay, I have him. A *mentsch*, a good soul. Ready to take on a leading role at last. You've written many scripts with this one."

"That's part of the attraction. I never have to explain myself to Charles and he's incredibly dependable. I can't tell you how many times he's rescued me. When my parents went bankrupt and killed themselves … after my husband left me pregnant with our second child."

Suicide. Abandonment. Mira's story wasn't half as impressive.

"I meant in more realities than this one," Rhonda said. "If your world didn't go so *meshuge* over time, you'd realize a thousand years are like yesterday. He has always been with you and, sometimes, you've done the rescuing. So what's the problem?"

"It feels too easy," Angel said.

"Why create the belief that life must be difficult?"

"I haven't proved I can make it on my own yet. I can't pay my bills on time and I've got zero savings for a house or the boys' education. Marrying Charles would solve all that, but – don't laugh – you know what stops me? Wondering what Gloria Steinem would say."

"Does Gloria pay half the rent, roast you a chicken now and again, baby-sit?"

Angel laughed. "No."

"You think from fasting you'll get rich?"

"No, but that's not all. Charles has a weak heart. I don't know how long he'll live."

"So, maybe the contract calls for him to disengage first. People come, people go."

"Why make contracts you know will cause pain?" Angel asked.

"Pain, schmain. We're not talking root canal or childbirth, right? So he leaves. An actor exits the stage when he runs out of lines. You forget you are eternal. You create the idea of death – and it is only an idea – to move things along. It's not for nothing you wrote this script."

"What I want to know is if marriage is part of the script, part of the contract I've made with Charles."

"Look for the story you're telling each other and you'll have your answer. Who's next?"

Angel flopped back in her chair, clearly exasperated. The others brought up problems at work, problems at home, mysterious aches and pains.

"People!" Rhonda said. "You're such vinegar pusses tonight. Life is supposed to be fun. These plays you've written for yourselves? Get into them. Go for an Oscar."

"It annoys the heck out of me when she won't give you the answer," Angel said on the way home.

"Don't you find her Yiddish accent a bit odd?" Mira asked.

"Not at all. She said her last planting – well, last in the way we think of last – was in Jewish soil. Isn't that wonderful? She's role playing like she says we all do. The other channellers I tried all spoke like Polish counts."

In Mira's opinion, Rhonda hadn't said anything Jackie couldn't have made up. It didn't make sense that Angel would spend ten bucks a week on so-called study group yet drive with a broken muffler. "Has Jackie been tested?"

"For what?"

"There must be some voice test. She *sounds* different as Rhonda but maybe she's just a good actress. And that talk about scripts. I don't want to piss you off, but it's hard to believe."

Angel reached over and lightly touched Mira's arm, her touch like a secret passing between them. "You won't offend me by speaking your mind, Sweetie."

Mira had never thought of herself as a Sweetie. She liked it.

"As far as I know," Angel said, "God hasn't been tested, either, and look how many people believe in him or it or her. All I know is God doesn't talk to me. Rhonda does. She's helping me discover my soul's mission. There's nothing more important than that. If I knew for sure marrying Charles was part of that mission, I wouldn't hesitate. But I don't, and I can't afford another mistake."

Mira had never spent two minutes thinking about her soul, much less its mission. "Did she tell you where your parents are?" She wondered for a crazy moment if Rhonda could reach Marko.

"No. If I wanted her to find anyone, it would be my ex so I could

121

sue for support. But she needs a location. Heck, if I had that, *I* could find him."

Angel's ex didn't see the kids, didn't have a clue what Matty even looked like. He'd won a bunch of money gambling and didn't want to share it.

"What a sleaze," Mira said. She and Marko had "won" a decent inheritance and shared it freely until it was gone.

"Fine for Rhonda to say, 'people come, people go.' I have to think about the boys. What if they get attached to Charles and he dies before they're grown? Anthony was a mess for two years after his father left. I wish someone would just tell me what to do. Not having to worry about money would be heaven. Is it terrible to want more than I have?"

"I'd still be in Edina if I could afford it."

"I wondered about that."

"My brother and I were living together and he died. I couldn't handle the rent on my own." There. She'd said it without getting weepy.

"Oh, Mira. How? When?"

"April. A fish bone in his esophagus. He couldn't turn his neck that night without it hurting but he was too macho to go to emergency. He went to bed and never woke up."

Angel sucked in her breath. "An infection that went to his lungs."

"Yes." Mira swallowed hard and turned her head towards the window, watched the stars play hide-and-seek between the buildings rushing by. When she could speak again, she said, "You know that restaurant on the corner of Fourth and Seventh?"

"No, is it any good?"

"I don't recommend the stuffed trout."

Angel shook her head. "Oh, Sweetie, I'd like to give you a big hug right now."

Mira sniffed the apartment air that night for Marko's scent: a mix of Brut and garlic pickles. She tried to imagine him lurking in the wings like some celestial Peeping Tom, waiting for new lines. If the couches and tables were merely props in a play they'd written, it wasn't fair that the set had a longer life than he did. It looked like a doctor's waiting room now. Nothing personal about it at all. "Curse you, Red Baron," she said, raising a fist to the ceiling. "Even if we did have a contract." Without cash to replace the furniture, she wondered how she could change the set.

She unpacked a few cartons, looking for inspiration. Their baseball equipment, her sketch-books, the pastel and watercolour pencils. In a book box she found the dictionary. Disengage: *to detach, free, loosen or separate.* Animus: *in Jungian psychology, the masculine aspect of a woman's personality.*

She had taken a psychology course in university but all she retained from it was an image of the professor rocking back and forth in front of the class, rubbing himself against a hard-backed chair. It occurred to her she might have wasted those years, helping Marko with his exams and papers, spending only enough time on her own to pass. Angel was on a quest for her soul's mission. What could Mira claim to be doing? She'd gone after her new job simply because it paid more. Nothing creative about it. She didn't even get to write the commercials. If she could stick it out long enough to put some money aside, she'd take an art class or two. She felt a surge of new ambition.

The program from a play she and Marko had seen at the Guthrie turned up in one of the boxes. *Cyrano.* She had loved everything about it but he'd called it a big yawn. There was a balcony in that play. She had a balcony.

"Just macaroni and cheese," Angel had said when she called, "but I'd love some grown-up company." As the elevator was on the fritz, Mira took the fire stairs and made her way down the dimly lit hallway to 103. A pack of kids nearly knocked her over. Marko would've insisted on an adults-only place.

Angel opened the door wearing black leggings, a billowy white blouse and no makeup. Could anyone be that pure?

Mira had lugged along two gloves, a bat, a couple of balls. "I thought we could give the boys a work-out after supper, help you release some of that animus."

Angel laughed then made a face. "I'm hopeless at baseball."

"I'll help you."

Angel's apartment was laid out like Mira's except it had a second bedroom and a small concrete slab patio. She led Mira through the galley kitchen into the dining area. "Come sit with me. We'll eat when their show's over." The boys were on the living room floor in front of the TV, stuffing potato chips into their mouths. Their little hunched backs looked harmless enough.

Angel cleared a pile of mail off a chair for Mira. "I only open the ones that say Final Notice on the envelope."

Her living room looked like a set from *South Pacific:* white wicker furniture with rose and beige cushions, pictures of pink and white shells on the walls. "Is that real?" Mira asked, pointing to a six-foot palm tree next to the patio door.

"Doesn't it just look it? It's silk. A gift from Charles. He'd pay my bills if I let him, but I won't, so he surprises me with things I'd never buy: a leather dress, of all things, a huge box of walnuts – like I bake. There's a carousel horse in my bedroom." She walked to the tree as if on springs. "Have you ever noticed that a gift carries the electromagnetic energy of the person who gave it to you?"

"Can't say I have." An image of Charles was coming to her: Mr. Moneybags in top hat and spats, dancing around a *Monopoly* board.

"I tried it in several different places before it worked. Same as a real plant. A plant's consciousness responds better to one area than another even if conditions are the same." She moved her hand slowly around the tree, not touching the fronds. "I feel little bubbles of carbonation. Little bubbles of Charles's subconscious."

"What's the point?"

"Connection. One soul essence connecting with another. Connection is everything." She twirled around like a child with her arms out then leaned down and hugged the boys.

"Hey!" Anthony said. "You're making me miss the best part."

"Well, excuse me," Angel said. She came back to the table, flushed – from motherly connection, Mira supposed. Mira didn't know the first thing about plants or children.

They talked about Charles. His parents were diplomats who'd left him so well off he'd never had to do anything except keep himself busy. They died when Charles was in his twenties. When he wasn't travelling, he played piano until his fingers ached.

"He's had a stutter for as long as I've known him," Angel said, "but when he plays, I could weep for what his fingers are able to say."

Mr. Moneybags, flipping his tux tails up and over the bench, sitting down to play something staccato. "Do you love him?"

"Love's one of those vague words. I'm enormously fond of him. He's fun. Always on, always performing. Trying to distract everyone from the stuttering. Sad, really, but also endearing. He says I'm the only woman who's never treated him as if he's brain damaged."

"You wouldn't marry him because of that, would you?"

"I'm never quite sure what I'll do. I try to stay away from cliffs for that reason."

Mira laughed because Angel did, but she wasn't sure Angel was kidding.

Angel and the boys saw Charles three or four times a year. "He's coming for Thanksgiving. You must meet him. He stays in a hotel when he's here, proper to a fault. Flies us out to his place when I can take the time off. His house, you should see his house! Overlooking the ocean. I have such *longing* there."

"For what?'

"To be a drop in that ocean, hugging all the other drops as we crash onto the shore. If I didn't have the boys, I would find a deserted island and do nothing but meditate, become a wave in my mind. Let me show you something." She took down a picture that was taped to the refrigerator and brought it back to the table. A townhouse development. "Look at all the land around it. In the winter you can cross-country ski right outside your front door. I'd have to sell tons more than I do now for a place like that. Put more hours into it than I can manage with the boys."

Mira felt dizzy trying to fathom what Angel truly wanted. "Having that house would make you feel like a wave?"

"I never thought of that. Aren't you clever? Maybe. A powerful wave. Powerful enough to provide for my boys."

"I'm off work at four Tuesdays and Thursdays," Mira said. "I could pick them up and feed them those days. You could work as late as you wanted."

Angel put her hands over Mira's. "What a treasure you are."

"I'm hungry," Matty wailed. Their show was over.

At dinner, Anthony was quiet and watchful. The moody one, like Marko. Then Matty made farting sounds with the ketchup bottle and got Anthony laughing so hard, food came out his nose. Angel lifted up her hands in mock despair and said, "Boys. What can you do?"

"Don't let them bamboozle you," Mira said.

"What's boozle?" Matty asked.

"Tricking people. I had a boozler brother. I know all the tricks."

Anthony blew on his fist and studied Mira.

"I don't want any more," Matty said, pushing his plate away.

"How 'bout I make you spaghetti and meat balls on Tuesday?" Mira said.

"I don't like meatballs," he said.

"I'll put them on the side."

Anthony took his fist away from his mouth. "Can you cook it here? Nothing to do at your place."

"How do you know? I might have every set of baseball cards since 1957."

"Do you?" Anthony's expression hovered between mistrust and hopefulness.

"You'll have to come up and find out."

Mira felt a weird and wonderful sense of purpose. If her soul had had a mission before, it could only have been to watch over Marko and she'd blown that. She'd been given a second chance with Angel – the boys, too, even though she had no maternal stirrings. On Tuesdays and Thursdays, she ferried them home from the sitter's in the Mustang, the top down, smiling at the sight of them in the rear view mirror, hair whipping around their faces. She filled their tummies. She recruited them in transforming her living room into a set for *Cyrano*. Draped the furniture with sheets and covered the carpet with drop sheets; covered the boys with Marko's work shirts; set paint, brushes, and water jars on the big glass coffee table. A forest began to form on either side of the sliding glass door to the balcony. She had sketched floor-to-ceiling trees on the wall and let the boys loose to fill them in with green leaves and blue leaves or no leaves at all. Trees with funny faces and scary faces. Trees bearing squirrels, apples, and birds.

"You're looney," Angel said. "The management will have your hide."

"I can always paint over it," Mira said. "Or maybe I'll tell them what Rhonda would say: the trees are there and not there at the same time."

Mira told Anthony and Matty the story of the large-nosed poet who courted the beautiful Roxane on another's behalf, even though the poet, himself, was secretly in love with Roxane. Except for the part about the duel, the story bored them until Mira bought them rubber noses to wear while they painted.

Angel said she'd never felt so supported, that Mira was what she imagined a sister would be. Mira wondered if Angel was what a best friend was supposed to be. She'd only ever had Marko, never a close girlfriend. They started eating most suppers together, pooling their grocery money, amazed at how cheaply they could eat with imagination and planning. To save even more, Mira gave up study group – not a big sacrifice – and Angel limited herself to every other week.

After Anthony and Matty were in bed each night, they'd sit side by side on Angel's floor, their backs against the couch, keeping their voices low. Angel would talk about her dreams for the boys. How her desire to do right by them was almost a physical ache. Mira told Angel about the paintings that formed in her sleep and scribbled their way onto notepads and blotters at work. All that marred Mira's happiness was the spectre of Charles's visit and that was a long way off. He called Angel every Wednesday night at seven but the calls were short.

Three weeks before Thanksgiving, Angel showed up early at Mira's, her green eyes puffy from crying. "I could hardly see the road for my tears," she said at the door. "Where are they?"

"In the living room playing *Parcheesi*."

"I don't want them to see me upset, don't want them asking questions."

Mira took Angel in her room and quietly closed the door.

"They've changed the commission structure," Angel said. "The top ten percent will make twenty percent more, the rest twenty percent less. It's heartless, Mira, so heartless." The change was effective December first. Her regional manager had handed out motivational cassette tapes the sales reps were supposed to play in their cars to and from appointments. Angel's car didn't have a cassette player.

Mira gave Angel a consoling hug, but hopeful ideas were afloat in her head. "Take the Mustang," she said. "And we can rent a three-bedroom together. Only forty dollars a month more than what you're paying all by yourself."

Angel lifted her eyebrows in surprise.

"I've been thinking about it for a while," Mira said. "I checked it out."

Angel smiled weakly. "You're so sweet, you really are, but this must be the sign. I drove out to the river today, walked the path. The wind was bitter, already, and we're still weeks from winter. I thought about how warm California is all year. And how meaningless my work is: trying to interest busy doctors in a brand. Charles will need a nurse one day. It's the least I can do for him. I called him before I came upstairs. He's flying out this weekend to talk it over."

Mira sat down hard on the edge of her bed. "Why didn't you ask me first?"

"Your permission? You're kidding, right?"

"For help. Why didn't you ask me for help?"

"You're as poor as I am. Where's the percentage in that?"

Mira got up and opened the door. "I'll tell the boys you're here. And wrap up the leftovers for you. We had Meat-za Pie. I hid mushrooms under the cheese and Matty ate them."

She sat in the dark for hours that night, passing a flashlight beam back and forth across Cyrano and Roxane's forest. It had brought tears to Angel's eyes when it was finished. "Their little souls are all over that wall," she had said. Mira replayed other conversations, looking for where she'd read too much into Angel's words. The next day she booked a private session with Rhonda. Seventy-five dollars on her credit card for advice from what was probably only Jackie's imagination.

"What do you believe you deserve?" Rhonda said. "What you believe is what you'll get."

Mira had to think about whether she felt herself deserving of anything. "More time, I guess. To show Angel she has options. She's giving up too soon."

"What is she giving up, exactly?"

Mira had to think again. "Me," she said softly.

"So schlep yourself out to California, continue your friendship there."

"It wouldn't be the same. I'd have to share her with Charles."

"Aha, okay, the heart of the matter. Listen. Here comes a clue. It's not a coincidence you three have come together. A play you wrote in another life is having a revival in this one."

Mira listened, incredulous, as Rhonda told her that she, Angel, and Charles plunged to their deaths while climbing the Alps in the seventh century. They were close friends, young men all, eager for adventure before settling down. It wasn't their first expedition. Charles had someone waiting for him and he'd promised her it would be his last. Angel had chosen the mountain face the three would climb that day. Mira had been as aimless as "a fart in a barrel," as Rhonda expressed it, willing to let the others write her lines.

"What *should* I have done?" Mira asked.

"There's no should or shouldn't," Rhonda said. "There just is."

"Was Marko on that mountain, too?"

"No, he is your sister in that life and she has the same birthmark you do now. Then, as now, you believe one of you has to exit for the other to star."

"Where is my birthmark?" Mira asked.

"I don't play parlour games. You choose to believe or not." Unless something unforeseen happened, Rhonda said, the probability was for Angel to marry Charles. Mira would have to be content knowing she and Angel had deeper relationships in other realities.

But this is who I am now, Mira thought, and now is all I can be content with.

Charles arrived that Friday. "He wants to meet you," Angel said when she called to invite Mira to dinner the following night. "Please say yes."

Seconds after Mira knocked, a tall, balding man with a barrel chest flung open Angel's door. Balancing wire-rimmed glasses on the edge of his long nose. Over his charcoal wool suit – hadn't Angel said casual? – he wore a navy blue bib apron that shouted *Cocktails with Charles* in orange letters. He handed Mira a little napkin that said the same.

"C-c-care to try my special mmmartini?"

"Why not?" Mira said. She'd had two fortifying beers at her place and was feeling loose. She stepped into the kitchen, steamy from whatever was in the oven. Angel lifted her gaze from the green peppers she was chopping, a wary look. Mira kissed her soapy-scented cheek and said, "Smells great." Angel gave her a grateful smile.

"Where did you find that apron?" Mira asked Charles. "And the napkins?"

He'd had them custom made, Charles said, in anticipation of meeting Mira at Thanksgiving. Luckily, they were ready early.

"I'm flattered."

"He's been driving me batty getting ready for you," Angel said. "Commandeered half the counter space for his bar." She smiled indulgently at Charles, and Mira could see something pass between them, a history she couldn't match – in this life, anyway.

"I'll stand over here, then, out of the combat zone," she said, sidestepping her way to the dining area. "Been to the storage locker, I see." The table was set with a sky blue cloth, tall white candles, and china Mira had never seen. Only a week ago, she and Angel, famished and lazy, had sat there eating leftover chili straight out of the pan.

"Food tastes so mmmuch better when you take time to set a p-p-proper table," Charles said. He was mashing mint leaves, lime juice, and brown sugar with a wooden thingamajig he called a muddler. He'd had one foot out the door, he stammered, before he remembered to slip it into his carry-on case. He was gesturing so widely he almost whacked Angel in the head.

What Mira would soon have in her hand, he said, was *La Mojita*, a drink he learned to make from a Cuban exile in Miami. "Angel was kind enough – p-p-patience personified," he said, to drive him around that morning to find the fresh ingredients he needed. He had purchased the vital raspberry twist vodka in California, not wanting to leave that to chance. Because of his condition, he'd have his with juice. Mira must tell him what she thought of the real thing. Would she care to join him in the living room? What a scriptwriter this Charles was.

"I *love* this drink," Mira called after him. The first sip had gone right to her head and she was softening towards him. Imagining him in lederhosen. Angel had cleaned up the place. It was usually littered with newspapers, GI Joes, unopened mail, and abandoned mugs with half an inch of cold tea in them. Mira watched Charles ponder where to sit before he landed on the couch next to the phoney palm. He seemed to swallow the space. The boys – more scrubbed and subdued than usual – were on the floor playing *Battleship*. Matty gave her a smile she wished Angel could see.

"Hey, boozlers," she said, lowering herself to the floor beside them, careful not to spill her drink, aware that she wasn't in total control.

"B-b-boozlers?"

"Private joke," Mira said and winked at the boys.

Angel entered the room carrying a five-string banjo emblazoned with a gold eagle on the back. It must have been three feet tall.

"Look what Charles brought us." She took a seat beside him.

"I didn't know you played banjo," Mira said.

"We don't. Yet. Charles bought an extra plane ticket so he could keep it on the seat next to him." She patted his knee. "He's too much."

Charles beamed and burst into loud song, "I come from Monterey-yay with a banjo on my knee." Not a single stutter.

Anthony and Matty exchanged smirks.

"So, when were you in Miami?" Mira asked, hoisting her *La Mojita* in Charles's direction.

"Mmmany times."

"Charles manages his own investments," Angel said. "He likes to visit the companies he invests in."

"Do you play much baseball?" Mira asked him.

Charles looked appalled, as if she'd asked if he did much dope. "I wwwasn't well as a ch-ch-child," he said. "Nnnot much time for sports."

Angel jumped in to say he'd had rheumatic fever as a child and it had damaged his heart. Medication seemed to be doing the trick for now, although his doctor had mentioned the possibility of valve surgery, something Angel intended to discuss with that doctor. Her voice had clothed itself in a nurse's uniform already.

"The reason I asked about baseball," Mira said, tripping over the words in a haste to reinsert herself, "is that Matty's into T-ball and Anthony has been kicked up to the majors. The regular season was over by the time I moved in. I was planning to give them a good work-out between games next summer." Rhonda had said to go for an Oscar, but first you had to win the part.

Angel gave Mira a look. Mira gave her one back that said, What? and swallowed the rest of her drink.

"Mira throws like a boy," Anthony said to Charles.

"Correction. I'm a girl, so I throw like a girl."

"If all goes as p-p-planned," Charles said, "We'll be taaaking the boys to the Oakland games. Season t-t-tickets."

We.

"Boo, Oakland, boo," Anthony said.

"That's rude," Angel said, giving him a stern look. "You'll get to see the Twins when they play Oakland."

"Neat," Matty said.

Anthony narrowed his eyes.

"So, Charles," Mira said, her mouth starting to feel mushy. "I'm curious. Why marry now, after all those carefree bachelor years?"

Angel stood abruptly, throwing Mira a cautionary look. "I'd better check on dinner. Time to wash up, boys."

"Huh?" Matty said. Something new. The boys furrowed their brows and looked at Mira. She grinned and nodded towards the bathroom. They stood and slunk away.

Mira turned back to Charles. "Well?"

He slid off the couch and onto the floor next to her. "Mmmay I confide?" he asked in almost a whisper. "All mmmy life I have been afraid to taake a risk. Afraid to mmmake a mistake. I ww-want to d-d-do something worthwhile bee-fore it's too late. Adopt the b-b-boys. Give them my nnname."

Mira wondered what was wrong with the name they had, but she was touched by his candour. She felt singled out and trusted. It made her believe he really *had* gotten the apron and napkins just for her. *I wish I could remember you.*

"Will you light the candles, Charles?" Angel said from the edge of the kitchen. Had she overheard?

Charles struggled to his feet. "Cer-er-tainly. Have they been lit beee-fore?"

"No, they're brand new."

"Then why don't I taaake them into the hallway and b-b-burn them for a mmmoment?"

"Whatever for?"

He explained it was good manners to burn a new candle briefly in advance of a dinner party so the offensive smell of first snuffing would be out of the house when guests arrived. Since Mira was already there, he could accomplish the same objective by pre-lighting the candles in the hallway.

"How interesting," Angel said. "Mira, will the smell of new candles offend your senses?"

Mira stood with a grunt. "Hell, no. I'll even go out in the hallway and burn them with you, Charles." He lit the candles where they were and gave Mira a rueful smile.

"So mmmany p-p-points of protocol I learned helping my p-p-parents entertain," he said. "I mmmistakenly assume others know them, as wwwell."

Angel squeezed his arm and said, "It's okay. Even after all these years, we have lots to learn about each other."

The boys came back and took their chairs. "What's the yucky stuff in the rice?" Matty asked. Anthony snickered.

"Honestly," Angel said. She picked up a bottle of wine from the table. "A gift from Charles for you and me," she told Mira, filling their glasses. Charles was having water, the boys something orange.

"Then I shall have to make a toast," Mira said. Angel's eyes widened.

"To all the lives we've ever lived," Mira said, lifting her glass, "and all we ever will." She took a big sip.

Angel smiled. "Lovely."

"Hear, hear," Charles said.

Anthony said, "I don't get it."

They tucked into the meal, almost every bite punctuated by Charles exclaiming how exquisite it was. Mira had never seen anyone hold silverware that way. He didn't shift his fork from his left to his right hand once.

"Which one of us went over the mountain first, do you suppose?" she said, looking to Angel and Charles in turn.

Charles gave her a questioning smile.

Angel said, "Pardon?"

"Just thinking about something Rhonda said. The Alps? Ode-layheehee," she sang.

The boys laughed but Angel looked perplexed, even a little annoyed.

"Guess you had to be there," Mira said. She smiled at the boys sitting across from her. Her heart felt empty and full at the same time. People kept slipping out of her hands.

"Don't pick up the asparagus with your fingers, Matty," Angel said.

Mira got up, walked around to Matty's place and cut his asparagus into small pieces.

"He has to learn to do that on his own," Angel said, an edge to her voice.

Mira returned to her chair, replaced her napkin on her lap and locked eyes with Angel. "Do you enjoy robbing me of everything?"

Angel looked shattered. Charles coughed and Anthony said, "What?"

Mira studied her plate until the boulder in her throat crumbled. "I really miss my brother," she said and stood. "Sorry for spoiling your evening." She made it to the door quickly and stepped into the hallway. Angel was right behind her.

"Tell me what's happening. I'm tense, I know. Sorry if I took it out on you. Should I walk you upstairs?"

Mira stood facing the wall opposite Angel's door. "I'm fine. It's not your fault we fell off the mountain, you know. I should have paid more attention."

Angel stepped closer and let out a long, slow breath Mira felt on her neck. "Mira, I don't know what you're talking about."

"Of course you don't and that's what's so hard to bear. We go through all these lives together then move on. A curtain drops across our memories each time, like we never existed before."

Angel put her hands on Mira's shoulders. "Sweetie, you will always exist for me."

They would both say later they didn't know how it happened. As Mira turned around, their faces were only inches apart. Angel's breath had a fruity smell. Her mouth was as soft as fresh bread. It was a light kiss at first but accompanied by tremors of recognition. Mira was surprised she didn't want to kick herself around the block later. Angel would say she felt little bubbles of Mira's consciousness for hours.

Angel called early the next morning. "I told him I won't leave you."

"What did he say?"

"That his house is more than big enough."

The Snow People: 30-46 AGM

I sprang not / more in joy at first hearing he was a man-child / than in first seeing he had proved himself a / man.
—Volumnia in *Coriolanus*

ᏨᎦᏁᎠ

SELANNA

THIRTY YEARS AFTER THE GREAT MIGRATION

To the child in my womb I say: the blood passing between your heart and mine comes from the very first Snow People, two lovers who defied an ancient taboo and ate the liver of a polar bear. It should have killed them. Instead, it turned their skin and hair as white as the great bear's fur and their eyes the colour of a glacial lake. The lovers had seven children, all with the same white skin and hair, all but one with the same startling eyes. For thousands of years, the lovers' white-skinned, white-haired descendants worshipped The Land and survived on what it bestowed until even the winter ice began to thin and fewer of the fish they caught and fewer of the animals they hunted passed their way. One year the ice refused to return, and water swallowed The Land. The Snows loaded up their boats and began the Great Migration south. After many seasons, they landed on an island populated by people the Snows called Rainbows in a republic called New Columbia. The Rainbows took their boats away and the Snows could no longer hunt and fish. They could no longer worship The Land.

30 AGM. The sun was everywhere that May afternoon, gloating at its triumph over months of relentless rain. Gruzumi and I flowed

out of the Village to collect with the others, like storm water, at the edge of the nature reserve – an undulation of alabaster bodies, most in mismatched clothes worn to softness, everything too short. We must have numbered a thousand. No more polite tugging on sleeves for promises of small gains. We were ready, at last, to reclaim the dignity of our elders.

Ada, as my mother insisted I call her, had stayed behind. "You'll earn us nothing but trouble, acting so big," she said earlier that day, leaning on the doorpost of the bedroom we shared, arms folded across her parrot-coloured blouse. Watching me step into the jumpsuit she'd made of black denim and striped cotton cadged from the recycling centre where she worked. No ill-fitting clothes for Adawalinda's daughter.

"You refuse to see all they do for us," she said. "They could put us on the street tomorrow, cancel our jobs, let us starve."

"You refuse to see their ignorance," I said, tucking my long, straight hair behind my ears in a way I knew she found too severe. I felt more powerful than she could imagine, bound to a mission I could not yet name. Reasoning with her was pointless.

"They'll drop you from the program," she said, lifting her dyed eyebrows into cartoonish frowns. "You can't have it both ways."

"I don't care," I said, which wasn't true. I was one of few Snows admitted into the Sustainable Skills teaching program. Like my grandmother, Aaka Elin, I could tell you which plants healed, which ones poisoned. In less than two years, I would finish my training and explain to my students why mackerel swam in our waters but salmon no longer did, how evening primrose seeds could ease pain, that each part of a dandelion was useful. My students. They populated my inner world already. I'd spawned their need for me and mine for them.

"We wouldn't starve," I told Ada on my way out the door.

The Rainbows didn't resent us at first. Visiting scientists needed meeting rooms, hotel beds, and restaurant meals while they tried to decode our genes. We attracted journalists and tourists who filled the streets almost year-round until I was six, before fuel surcharges kept away all but the wealthy and shut the ferries down. Some looked in shadowy doorways for Snows who didn't mind trading on curiosity about the colour of the hair between their legs. Others tugged at our heads, convinced we wore wigs. If they stroked my head, I'd purr loudly to embarrass them. I stared openly at the many shades of their hair and skin, the pink of their fingernails. Aaka Earth had decorated them from her full palette. Except for our eyes, we merited only a single hue.

"Never mind," Ada would say. "How boring if all butterflies looked alike." She was happy for the cash tourists paid to be photographed next to us, our bodies rising heads above theirs, like Douglas firs among Jack Pines. She spent it on deep red lipstick when there was still lipstick to buy.

"How do you tell each other apart?" tourists would ask.

I could spot Gruzumi a block away, that hip-rolling, unhurried walk I counted on to calm me. My hands, alone, would have known him by the mole on the back of his neck, where his long braid began, and the smooth strip of his spine where it ended, by the cool, metal disk encircling a hole in his earlobe big enough for my pinky to go through.

Arms around each other's waists, he and I burrowed into the crowd. Advised by an underground legal association, our Elder Council instructed us through red bullhorns that flashed in the sun: *Courage, Snows. Stand firm for justice, but don't resist arrest. Don't talk back.*

"The hell we won't," Gruzumi said.

Yeah. I pulled his face down and kissed his soft, pale mouth, brushed my nose across the strip of white fuzz edging his upper lip. He was my heart, pumping conviction into my veins as potent as any hallucinogenic fungus. I craved him more than justice.

In rows of locked arms, the sea of us flooded the streets leading to Parliament. At its last session before summer recess, New Columbia would vote on legalizing a long-standing practice: restricting us to government jobs that paid in credits instead of cash, credits we could use only for Village housing and in government stores. When the bill was proposed, we sent petitions and delegations to Parliament members. The Elder Council wrote letters to neighbouring republic Prairie Shield, asking it to intervene. Its silence on the matter led the more impatient of us to propose sit-ins and roadblocks, though we'd never tried them before, never stood up for ourselves even once. The Council's pitiful concession was a peaceful march. Snows couldn't vote. How would our mere presence persuade even a single politician to act on our behalf?

An honour guard of various ages led the way, hoisting placards that read *Bill 82: You Know It's Wrong* and *Snow Rights Are Human Rights*. Although our route had been well-publicized, a few microcars collected behind us, beeping their toy-like horns, expecting us to give way. I flipped them a mental finger. Snows weren't entitled to fuel rations, weren't supposed to travel beyond the electric shuttle range.

"Get out and walk, you bastards!" Gruzumi shouted.

A few cowards called out for him to shut up, to not make trouble.

In answer, I began chanting, "Bastards, bastards." Others joined in, and the chant morphed into "Faster, faster." It rolled across the crowd, gathering intensity and pulling us forward as if we were kites on the verge of lifting. The sky was a deep blue and the sun so brilliant it whitewashed the ground and painted our shadows in giant dark spikes. Oh to lie naked with Gruzumi under a billion suns! I felt giddy from all that light and sky; buoyant from having Right on our side.

A few "snow flakes" – what some Rainbows called those sympathetic to our cause – joined the march. Hostile others stood along the route holding their own placards: *What more do you want? Send the bloodless giants back*. In another age, we might have been as sacred as white tigers or stags. The white butterflies as prized as the swallowtails, coppers, and blues.

Half a dozen police flanked our march in air scooters that whined as they hovered and gargled when they flew back and forth. Hundreds more, on foot and in riot gear, waited at the Parliament buildings. They formed a living fence across the entrance: silent, black sentries with praying mantis heads. Others were posted across the street in front of the nine-metre high seawall that held back the steadily encroaching ocean.

Gruzumi's low, deep moan gave voice to my fears. We often saw police in such numbers on the library's holovision, but the images came from faraway lands where refugees from drought or violent storms amassed at border crossings, desperate for food and shelter. "How lucky we are," Ada would say for my benefit when we watched those images together, her mouth puckered like a doll's. "Handed so much without a struggle."

The unexpected sight of that many police made the crowd buckle. People called out, "What should we do?" Some turned in retreat. But the bullhorns urged us to proceed with the plan to occupy the Parliament grounds. Most of us did, spreading over the grass like a stain, keeping a wary distance from the police. Another people's song rose up from our throng: *Keep on a-walkin', keep on a-talkin', marching up to freedom land.* I could see the words enter Gruzumi's back and strengthen his resolve. We added our voices to the chorus that grew so sonorous I imagined it reaching the mainland. Then a rhythmic rumbling began, like winter rain pounding every gutter on every roof in the city.

"Sit, sit!" voices around us shouted. "They won't hurt us if we sit down!" The crowd began collapsing in surges like stricken tents. Once all of us were down on the grass, I could see that the rumbling came from the police who marched towards us, steadily, slowly, beating their shields with batons. They made no announcements, no request to disperse, just rained down on their shields. The noise rose up through the earth and into my legs and hips. I wrapped my arms around Gruzumi and closed my eyes, willing the sound to stop. It did, and Snows at the front started screaming.

Gruzumi stood and pulled me up beside him. The police were swinging their batons, connecting with heads and backs. People had their hands up but still the police hit them as they waded through the crowd. We were far enough back to escape, and many around us rose and headed for the street, yelling for others to get out of their way, stepping on the hands of those still sitting as though stupefied.

"Stop!" Gruzumi shouted, waving his arms. "We outnumber them. If we run towards them, we can beat them back." Yes, but how many had heard?

"Beat them back, beat them back," I shouted over and over. The idea caught hold with others who tried to help turn the tide of retreating bodies, but we were too few. We grabbed hands and threaded our way upstream. I took the lead, lowering my head and stiffening my body to force us through. As we got nearer the screaming, it intensified. Then, a crackling and the smell of burnt toast.

"Sela, no!" Gruzumi said. He saw the dancing blue lightning before I did and tried to pull me back. It was as if foot-long knives ripped me apart. I fell on my face and went into convulsions. My jaw shook so hard I was sure my teeth would shatter. Struck, too, Gruzumi fell beside me. I felt his spasms through the ground. Even as the knife-like pain gave way to a fire burning inside me, I was aware of him and thankful we would die together.

By the time we pulled ourselves up on trembling arms and knees, the sun had painted the sky with purple and yellow streaks. Moaning bodies lay nearby. A stench assaulted my nose. I lowered my head and looked between my legs. Like a helpless infant, I had soiled myself.

"Can't take you anywhere," Gruzumi said. I tried to laugh for his sake. We rolled onto our backs and wept up into the bruised sky. When our tears were spent and we could speak again, we promised ourselves to each other for as long as forever would last.

"What have you done to us?" Ada said, when I returned to the Village. Emotion exposed the blood vessels under her cheeks. "Did they take down your code?"

Stamped on a metal tag around my neck was D-121782: building D, unit 12, resident 1782 in the Good Neighbour Village.

"No," I said, hurrying past her to our small washroom.

She pursued me. "What's that stink? What did you sit in? You've ruined that outfit."

I switched on the hydro, cupped my hands and scooped water into my mouth, trying to flush away the chemical taste at the back of my throat. That and my shameful smell made me want to retch.

"I'm disappointed in you," she shouted through the bathroom door.

Ada had been living my future since I entered university. "When we're teaching," she'd say, "we'll buy a sewing machine." Teachers received more purchasing credits than most. She made all our clothes, fusing a discarded skirt to a sweater, a sleeveless shell to a pair of pants, hand stitching them – every item an original, each with a story to tell. She dreamed of selling her designs to Rainbows. Adawalinda's Revivals, she would call them. I wanted her to be more than a beggar. But I wanted her to dream for us all.

I stripped and squatted over the toilet to clean myself. Gruzumi had gone off to prepare his parents. How to tell Ada he and I couldn't bear to be apart now, each afraid the other would disappear. Snows didn't get married as Rainbows did. We just decided to stay together. If I had my own room, Gruzumi could have moved in with us, but he wouldn't have fit into Ada's world of two.

"We're like orphaned sisters," she would say as we mopped up after storms or foraged in the dark during the rolling blackouts. Her father and brothers had perished during the Great Migration, leaving only her and Aaka Elin, whose body rejected the island diet for good when I was twelve. Ada had never lived with a man as an adult, not even the one who fathered me in 11 AGM when she was seventeen. Rumour held he was a tourist she met while telling fortunes down at the harbour, but she wouldn't talk about him and there was little Rainbow in me except for a few freckles – not unusual for a Snow – and a patch of pink skin on my right hip. I often wondered if the part of me that didn't understand her came from my father.

"Why are you punishing me?" she said as I packed my clothes

and Aaka Elin's sealskin pouch in which I kept dried herbs. "I believed in you before he did."

I tried not to hear her words or see her tears as I left for Gruzumi's apartment in the next building. Tried not to think of her talking in her sleep with nobody to hear.

Gruzumi's parents were behind one closed door when I arrived, his grandmother and sister behind another. "To give us time, alone," he said in a hushed voice as unfamiliar as his night clothes: wide-legged white pants and flowing white shirt.

The common room was dark except for one corner, lit from an ancient time. Floating candles encircled two embroidered cushions on opposite sides of a tray holding stone cups that had survived the Great Migration. The past cast an aura around the room, masking its shabby present.

"My mother made us tea," he said.

"Sprouted bread and jam, too," I said, so he'd know I noticed even though my gaze rarely left him. "Don't think I can sit. Feels like I'm bleeding, but there aren't any wounds."

"No," he said, "no evidence, no proof. Who will believe us?"

The wood floor groaned under his bare feet as he crossed it for more cushions. He made me a bed, helped me lie on one side. I watched him wince as he carefully kneeled, watched his calloused hands pour tea into the cups. His hair looked almost yellow in the candlelight. Should I have been serving him? A swallow of panic. I'd joined his family with barely a thought as to what my role would be. I raised myself onto an elbow and drank. Willow bark tea, sweetened with honey, the slightly bitter aftertaste promising to take my pain away.

"I thought I'd be left without you, shouldn't have put you in danger," he said. His shadow on the wall reached over to touch my cheek.

"We could have pushed them back if we'd planned it," I said.

"Not against shields of lightning. Next time it will be bullets."

The thought of a next time thrilled me. We had chosen the shields over retreat.

Later, in his room – mine too, now – we could only gently touch, our muscles as fragile as worn thread, but his body became my safe haven and I slept without dreaming.

I woke to Sunday morning light slipping through slatted blinds and the reverberating drone of a sky car flying low, rattling the windows.

"Mercenaries," Gruzumi said, from the edge of the bed, where he sat peering through the slats. My eyes stroked the fine, white hair on his shoulder. My Arctic wolf.

"The police must have brought them in," his father, Adero, said after we lowered our still sore bodies to the large, square mat in the main room. I was unaccustomed to eating on the floor. Ada and I used a small table and chairs rescued from the landfill.

Gruzumi's mother, Katsi, brought us bowls of soup of dried fish and spring greens. Afraid I'd spill the soup between the floor and my mouth, I waited until I saw Gruzumi's aaka, Pilipaza, and fifteen-year-old sister, Asalie, hold their bowls and spoons close to their mouths. No one seemed to expect anything of me at the moment. They were intent on the words Adero spoke with a hint of the old language: the sibilant sounds like drawn out zeds, my name an exotic "Zelanna."

"The police chief came on the radio. Said we threw rocks at his troops. Troops! We're at war now?"

"He's lying," Gruzumi said.

"Did he say they beat and shocked us?" I asked.

Pilipaza sniffed. "Of course not." At seventy, the bony-faced Pilipaza was one of the oldest Snows. Her status as Elder Council member earned Gruzumi's family a three-bedroom apartment. Her flat, unfriendly voice had always intimidated me even though her body was so bent, I could have toppled her with a finger. The next time we had fish soup, I'd add nettle greens for her thin bones.

"Thank you for the bread and jam last night," I whispered to Katsi who had sat on my left, "but I couldn't swallow anything except the tea." She smiled and gave my arm a quick, gentle squeeze. She was older than my mother with unapologetic lines radiating from the corners of her eyes. After several miscarriages, she'd had Gruzumi when she was twenty-nine and Asalie four years later.

"We need people to speak the truth," Adero said, the triangle of beard below his full lips moving up and down. He wore a tusk-shaped shell through his nose – only at home, to embarrass his children, he told me once. He kept fit maintaining the Village rainwater tanks, clambering onto roofs to clear leaves from gutters and check for drowned creatures: "four-legged, two-legged, winged ones," he said so many times Gruzumi would roll his eyes. A line from a child's verse, but I wondered if he'd ever actually found a two-legged one in the tank.

"What we need sooner is a new tag with the correct building and apartment code for Selanna," Pilipaza said, turning her full gaze on me for the first time. To all, she said, as if in proclamation, "Not a rock was thrown."

"Why are you so sure?" Katsi said. "We left before Sela and Zumi."

"Yeah, why did they zap *you*?" Asalie said, squinting at Gruzumi and me. She looked empty-headed with her faddishly sheared hair. I'd be teaching others like her before long.

I squinted back. "Nobody threw any rocks."

"The march was a mistake," Pilipaza said.

"It could have been better organized," I said, forgetting her role in it.

"When you're on Council, you can criticize. It was *too* well organized. We got a permit too easily, delivered ourselves into their hands. You just think about that."

All eyes turned to me. "When I'm old enough for the Elder Council, I hope it does more than issue ID tags, assign apartments, and beg the government to fix rotting wood and broken glass." You just think about *that*, I wanted to add.

Gruzumi made a show of kissing my hand and the others laughed, even Pilipaza.

"What's so funny?"

"You don't back down," Gruzumi said.

The rumble of heavy vehicles drew us from breakfast to the

wide front window. Quick-moving Asalie claimed the vantage point. Long, brown cargo trucks with fat wheels parked along the seawall across the street. Mercenaries from the republic of Mid-Norte spilled out. They levelled their rifles at Snows seated on the sidewalk in the traditional talking circles we called hoops. We'd seen the mercenaries before, but only in parades. In exchange for potable water, they were on call to protect us against invasion. Whatever they said made the Snows stand, drop their heads like supplicants and hurry into their buildings. The previous day's humiliation burned through me like a fever. I wanted blue lightning to spurt from my fingertips, cut through the glass, and knock the soldiers to the ground.

"I remember the day we were herded into these buildings," Pilipaza said, her voice more numb than flat. "No more cooking fires. No more boats. We accepted everything."

"Isn't that your mother, Sela?" Asalie said.

I squeezed in beside her, pressed my forehead against the glass, and peered down. Pointing up in our direction was Ada. Although the soldier next to her was tall, he had to look up at her face. Had she been in a hoop? She detested that custom, claiming it tried to keep a doomed past alive. To her, nothing worth mentioning had happened before today unless it had happened to the Rainbows.

"She's turning us in," Asalie said.

"What for?" Katsi said.

"For marching."

"She'd have to turn in half the Village, then. She probably wants Sela."

The soldier must have asked for Ada's ID because she pulled out her tag. If she didn't always wear that dark blue jumpsuit on her Sunday morning scavenges through refuse bins, I'd have sworn she had deliberately dressed like the mercenaries. The soldier waved over another who consulted a palmtop and shook his head. He gestured towards my mother's building. Ada stomped a foot and waved her arms about. A ridiculous sight that stabbed me with pride.

"I better go down," I said.

"I will," Adero said, putting a restraining hand on my arm. "Your tag. They might not let you back in here."

By the time Adero made it outside, Ada was sitting on the sidewalk, arms obstinately folded. Three mercenaries stood over her, conferring. When Adero approached, they stepped back quickly. One levelled his gun. Adero put his hands up. Another pulled the tag out from under Adero's shirt.

"It's that travesty in his nose," Gruzumi said. "They probably think it's wired."

Only Asalie laughed. No one mentioned the disk in Gruzumi's ear.

When Adero returned, his face was tight. "They wouldn't let me talk to her. We must apply to the police for permits, now, to assemble outside and to enter any building we don't live or work in. They have a machine with our codes in it."

"A palmtop," I said. "Embarrassingly old technology, my fellow students like to say, but it's more than *we* have."

"We talk to each other, not machines," Adero said, as if our deprivation was by choice.

Rainbows found the way we talked to each other unsightly: out in the open, in hoops. But sitting on the ground showed our respect for Aaka Earth and our responsibility to each other. The sight of Ada on the ground took me to task. I had brushed her aside like a cobweb.

"They can't keep us from the gardens," Pilipaza said. "I'm going to weed the asparagus. Others on the Council may have the same idea."

It was the law for all, even the Rainbows, to grow food for the government to harvest and sell back to us. Except for Parliament's ceremonial lawns, each patch of grass, every swimming pool, and all but a few parking lots had been converted into communal gardens or habitat refugia. The earth around the Village had been parcelled into plots, each apartment responsible for one.

We watched Pilipaza appear below with her trowel and heavy gloves, watched her show her tag to a soldier who waved her on to the plots at the back of the building. Ada rose and followed her. Later, Pilipaza said she had invoked Elder Council privilege and ordered Ada to join her in the garden. "She misses you," was all she would say about their conversation.

The soldiers left after a week, replaced by police officers checking tags at each entrance. Others in air scooters hovered over the sidewalk and streets, ensuring we got into the proper shuttles. Sky watchers. Helmeted birds of prey.

"Every vandal and bike thief must have floated out to sea," Adero said. "The police seem to have nothing else to do."

"They can't keep this up," Gruzumi said. "When they relax their guard, we should be ready."

To do what?

For weeks we woke expecting sympathetic Rainbows to speak out in outrage over our situation and the Elder Council to come up with a resistance plan. But the "snow flakes" were mute, and the Elder Council couldn't agree on a single action despite many meetings at the gardens. The matter-of-fact way Pilipaza reported their indecision clawed at my insides, Gruzumi's too. They needed more information, she said, needed us to gather intelligence about what Gruzumi began calling the Occupation.

At the desalination plant where Gruzumi backwashed filters and removed Asian green mussels that clogged the intake pipes, he learned the government had hired an advisor from Mid-Norte. A surge of immigrants from deluged Caribbean islands had made disruptive demands there and almost gotten away with it. At a different plant, Katsi ran a machine that filled and sealed pouches of drinking water for export. She heard someone say if there were fewer of us there'd be room for more skilled refugees from ravaged countries. Miracle makers, we laughingly called them, who'd resurrect a world of boundless water, food, and fuel.

I approached a student named Siri. Black hair, skin the colour of wild chanterelles. The closest I had to a colleague, having been paired with her in the food lab. I watched her enter the classroom and look around with a confidence only the Rainbows had, waited until she took a seat and slid in next to her. "Seems police headquarters has relocated to the Village," I said with a short laugh, as if it were inconsequential. "What have you heard about it?"

Lying next to Gruzumi that night I told him Siri had looked at her shoes when she said it cost a fortune to police our protest. Looked at the ceiling when she said her father told her they couldn't afford to let us get out of hand again.

"What's that mean, out of hand?" Gruzumi said, stroking my arm with his thumb.

"Blocking traffic, apparently, trampling the Parliament lawn – that shrine to turfgrass. She hadn't heard about the shields, and I could tell she didn't believe me."

Gruzumi looped an arm around me and pulled me over so my head was on his chest.

"Siri says we have it pretty good. Says, nobody gives them a home for nothing. When I told her we pay with our labour, she reminded me I wasn't working and didn't have to pay for the program like she did."

Gruzumi laughed when I told him I said it wasn't *my* fault she couldn't have a swimming pool. "Wait, there's more," I said. "When she said there's no room for anyone else because of us, I said anyone else would be better off migrating into space since most of the island will be under water soon. She looked scared, like she believes what they say about us being psychic, or is it psycho?"

Gruzumi was laughing harder, now, and I was laughing a little, too, but also crying, getting his chest hair wet.

"What is it?" he said.

"She didn't look at me once until I mentioned the island going under water."

"They never really see us, anyway," he said.

Ada showed up one evening, her arms full of books, laughing at the surprise on our faces.

"I thought you'd want these," she said. Poetry volumes I'd rescued from shredding. Other relics, too – big books with shiny pictures of pineapples and flowering ginger, rhinos, and penguins. Images of things I would never see. Pictures to show my children someday.

"I wasn't able to carry them all. I can bring more another time."

It had been a few weeks since I'd seen her and, then, only a quick visit in the gardens. Barefoot, my hair hanging loose, I wondered if I looked too much at home, if it would hurt her feelings. But her smile gave no such feeling away.

"The guard is gone from the lobby?" Adero said.

"No, no, I got a permit. Turn in your ID tag for this and you can go anywhere you want. They injected it with a syringe." Ada held out her arm to show us a disk, no larger than a grain of rice, embedded in the skin just above her left wrist.

"Welcome, Adawalinda," Katsi said. "Sit with us."

Ada had been to Gruzumi's before, but she made a show of looking for a chair. Adero set a cushion down for her between me and Asalie.

"Did it hurt?" Asalie said, lifting Ada's wrist to get a closer look.

"No, they rubbed something on it first. It was over so fast, I hardly noticed it."

"Why do we need it?"

"The reason they gave for the tags when we first got here," Pilipaza said, "was we only have one name, too many the same."

"It's called the Digital Guardian," Ada said. "It has my medical records in it. It's for our safety, the police explained. Some hospitals use them."

"Prisons, too," Gruzumi said.

"More efficient than a tag," Ada said. "You don't have to change it whenever you move."

"Yeah, because it tracks you," Gruzumi said. "They know where you are all the time. They know you're here."

"Can they use it to shock you?" I asked. My bowels were beginning to cramp.

Adero stood and reached a hand down to help Ada up. "You must go."

"Will I see you again?" Her lip quivered as her eyes pleaded with me. I knew she didn't understand.

I walked her to the door, wanting to hug her, but afraid of what it would do to us. "Maybe in the gardens."

For some time after Ada left, the silence was almost a presence needing its own cushion.

"I'm not getting one," I whispered, finally.

"Can they hear you in the bathroom?" Asalie said.

Gruzumi pounded his fist into his hand, one, two, three times. "We need to take to the streets, burn everything we can, make the air foggy from fire," he said.

"That is not our way," Adero said.

"No, our way is surrender," Gruzumi said, "but not for me anymore."

"Zumi," Katsi said, extending an arm out to him.

"Me either," I said, getting up, standing beside him.

"Did you know," Pilipaza said, "I once shot a goose from the sky?"

The next day on the shuttle I couldn't stop looking at wrists. Don't make a sound, I thought, but I couldn't have, anyway. Something had knocked the sounds out of me, sucked out all my breath. I opened the window next to my seat and used my hands to shovel air into my mouth, not caring if anyone stared.

I stumbled down the shuttle steps, but my legs refused to take me to class. Inching along the building, I looked this way and that, sure someone was watching. Palpitations threatened to burst through my chest. I breathed deeply and concentrated on my unreliable legs. Thought about running away, following the wind farms that traced the coast, finding a hollowed out tree in which to live, if such a tree existed. Can you leave someone and still be with him? I could see Gruzumi knee-deep in brine, ears throbbing from the roar of the desalination membranes at full power, missing me. I tried not to think of our promise, but it was always there, like a hand at the back of my neck. I would have to make myself as angry as he was, angry enough to be unafraid.

I slipped into the classroom, mouthing an apology for being late.

That night, my body was the hollowed out tree in which Gruzumi and I would live, my body our freedom. "It's so warm inside you," he said into my neck, and I knew I would not chew my morning after seeds.

31 AGM. To my newborn son, I say: your blood contains that of a man so courageous he took a knife to his wrist one night and dug out what they'd forcibly implanted. They sent him to prison on the mainland. I went a little crazy, I'm told. Ada came to live with us, to sleep on his side of the bed. When we got word he was dead, I would have died, too, if not for you. You filled me up, leaving no room for self-pity. The sheets were rusty with my blood when I pushed you out. You didn't cry. You landed in Pilipaza's hands all quiet and watchful. Your eyes were grey, your skin as pink as the patch on my hip, your hair more yellow than white. It's an omen, Pilipaza said. He is the One who will guide us. No, I said, we will do it together, Gruzumi's son and I. Katsi took the afterbirth out to the garden and returned it to Aaka Earth.

AKINTUNDE

He was nine when he first saw it in one of his mother's old books, and it made him catch his breath: a photograph of Earth, taken from the moon a hundred or so years before, great islands of land swimming in a single ocean and peeking through swirling white clouds. Alive, full of knowledge.

"Is it Aaka Earth?" he asked his grandfather.

"Yes and no," Aapa said. "The planet is only a shadow of Aaka Earth. Her spirit is the real world, not the one we see."

"Are we shadows?"

"So I was taught."

He had the vision after that: The Land's sparkling whiteness, clean and beautiful, rising from the ocean.

45 AGM. Akin and his mother crouch behind a fence across the street from a house they've been scouting for months. The last

occupied bungalow on a dead-end street in a dry part of the city. Two men in CONAV uniforms carry a body out to an ambulance: the old lady they haven't seen in weeks. A few small bumps under a sea-green sheet pulled up to cover her face. Akin imagines her skin stretched thin as a fly's wing, like Pilipaza's two years ago when he was twelve and Aapa Adero slipped her body into the ocean, a bundle of rocks to weigh it down.

CONAV won't be back for a few days, at least, to clean out the old lady's house and nail the doors and windows shut. The ambulance gone, he and Mother creep around the side of the house, past vines of deep purple tayberries covering the weathered picket fence. Akin tears off a few and crushes them on the roof of his mouth. Juicy, sharp. The rest of the garden has gone to weeds.

"We'll bring it back," Mother says. "May have to guard it when the trouble starts."

She means the chaos she expects when the last ship leaves the island and the Snows are on their own. The final evacuation of Rainbows, except for the deathly ill, is any day now, she's sure, though there's been no announcement and Rainbows have been fleeing the island for years. "Anyone can see tomorrow if they don't lie to themselves about today," she told him. "I knew when your father didn't come home from work that day I'd never see him again." Gruzumi, always Gruzumi. Akin never thinks of him as Father.

Except for the colour of the stucco and the occasional addition, every house on the street is the same. The back door leads to the basement and is locked from inside with a horizontal cross-hatch. Mother slides a crowbar between the door and the frame and lifts the hatch. "You this time?"

More a demand than a request, so he shrugs in agreement, though he should be the one standing guard. He's the one who can pass for Rainbow. But she keeps testing him, keeps trying to find more daring in him than he possesses. His name means *bravery returns* in some other language. Akintunde. A pathetic echo of Gruzumi.

She hands him the cloth sacks. "I'll get any tools in here and then be right outside," she says. "Listen for my signal that someone's coming."

Akin knows the drill. Go through the house quickly, no gawking. Take stuff they can eat, wear, or burn. No knickknacks, no furniture. Don't leave any drawer or cabinet so bare as to be obvious when CONAV comes back.

He tests the closed door at the top of the stairs to the main floor – unlocked – and hesitates for a long breath before pushing it open. All pets are supposed to be gone, shot by CONAV or let loose to run wild as game, but still. He steps into the kitchen and listens. Nothing. It reeks of death, but he won't mention that to Mother. She claims his imagination keeps him from noticing things that might endanger him. She'll insist he identify the source of the odour: mildew, rotting food, shit? Mother would say feces. The sea smells like hunger to him. To her, only of dimethyl sulphide.

The rooms are small and damp. He flicks a light switch. Dead. No generator to search for. He bags candles, holders, and matches. Hefts a large flashlight – it works! – and drops it into a sack. Cutlery, pots, and pans. Canned tomatoes. From the bathroom: towels, ointments, bandages, and precious, hard to find soap. By the front door: coats, rain boots, shoes, umbrellas. In a bedroom: blankets, sheets, underwear, sweaters, eye glasses, and half a dozen wooden frames with no pictures. The bed's unmade, probably where she died. Look for weapons, Mother said. He checks every drawer for a gun, kneels to see under the bed, lifts the mattress.

In the last room he sucks in a sharp breath at the wall of books. Imagines Mother fingering the covers, slowly turning the pages, looking for half-blank pages or wide margins. She's been scribbling poetry in her collection of old volumes since paper became scarce. Akin isn't the greatest reader but he's come across some of her sappy poems to Gruzumi from time to time. He flips through some books, bags four with white space.

"Look," he says as he lugs the sacks outside. "Empty frames." He pulls one out to show her. "They'll burn good."

She takes it, turns it around in her hand. "I don't have one picture of your father," she says like it was his fault. Sometimes he thinks he can't bear her loss another day.

She didn't finish school because of him. Ada told him that one day after he'd been mouthy. They dropped her from the program when she got pregnant with him. "You should show more gratitude." But even at his most grateful, he can never be Gruzumi.

His thoughts must slip away for a minute because Mother taps him on the arm. "Little boy," she says. "The neighbourhood's clear. Let's go."

She lugs a few bags to the fence, throws them over into the next garden. Akin does the same.

"The old lady had guts," he says, hoisting himself over the fence, "staying here by herself."

"Probably had no choice." Mother waves his hand away as she clears the fence, a lot of spring still in her legs.

"There's a chair by the fireplace I wish we could take."

"Too much comfort breeds a lazy mind," she says, then gives him her half-bitten, tight smile and squeezes his arm. She isn't serious. He's never sure.

They stow the bags in the house next door, one they commandeered months before. It's easy enough to pry the boards off a basement window; CONAV always does a half-assed job. They check around to be sure all is as they left it. Especially the big finds: fishing gear, four bicycles, two canoes, a kayak. Every house on the street now has liberated goods, waiting for them to move in. They'll share the houses with other Snows, but his family will be in charge, making sure everybody has something essential to do: gather wood, build fires, boil water, plant, weed, harvest. When the jobs disappeared, some people got sluggish and gave into worry. "They need work and routine to feel in control again," Mother says. She and Akin will give them that. Some days he wakes with a proud heart, anticipating how thankful they'll be.

Vacant houses closer to the Village are too soggy to live in, black smudgy water stains on the walls like dirty hand prints.

Their owners stripped them of the best stuff before the high water took them. During low tides, he and Mother pry up warped floor boards and take them to dry out in the houses they already think of as theirs.

On the way home, they stop for peas and strawberries at the hilltop garden, the closest one to the Village that isn't flooded. The vines are picked clean.

"Greedy bastards," Mother says. "They've lived like children too long. I almost welcome what's coming."

The government stopped harvesting when the waters rose. Mother expected the Elder Council to step in, but they've lost their voice. She calls them the Dead Ones.

From atop the hill they can see the ocean and water two metres deep that surrounds the Village like a moat, the wooden catwalks like drawbridges. They can see clear down to the harbour, too, and the fancy dome of Old Parliament sticking out of the water. Flooding will be worse come winter. Mother says it's due to atmospheric pressure and the relative positions of the earth, moon, and sun. But Akin believes the tide is freer to act than that. It has a greedy appetite, creeping in to eat away at bricks and plaster, leaving slimy green spit as it creeps out again.

"If we don't bring anything," he says, "they'll ask what we've been doing."

Mother doesn't appear to hear him. She's staring out at the ocean. "They never returned his body. How do I know he's dead?"

After Pilipaza died, he watched the ocean every day for months, half expecting the tide to bring her back. Hoping it would. When he had the vision about The Land, Pilipaza didn't say he imagined it. "My father's spirit journeyed where others' did not," she said. "You have his gift."

He would never watch for Gruzumi. What's so brave about digging a hole in your wrist? Maybe Akin will do the same one day if it impresses his mother so much. No one scans the stupid monitors anymore, anyway. The government's gone, the island handed over as a base for the naval forces of the Coalition of Pacific Republics. CONAV. His friend Zunar says it in a phoney deep voice, dragging out the second syllable – CONAAAV – and Akin pretends to tremble with fright.

Mother would say the room smells of bacteria and diet deficiency, but that afternoon it also smells of tension. Akin's family and another they took in when the first floor flooded – Zunar and his parents – sit on the common room floor, amid blankets, mattresses, and clothes. Zunar was in Akin's class before school closed for good. Mother calls him a fatuous boy. Akin doesn't know what that means, only that Zunar makes him laugh. He can't imagine Mother as a girl, having fun.

Everyone in the room but Akin fits together: white skin and hair, eyes so blue you can drown in them. If what Pilipaza told him was true, that his destiny is linked to the Snows' fate, why was he born with stained skin and eyes the colour of fog?

Aapa Adero waves them over almost absentmindedly, his face sagging with preoccupation. Akin squeezes in between Aapa and Zunar, who punches his arm and mouths, *Where were you?* Akin crosses his eyes and sticks out his tongue.

"CONAV was here," Aaka Katsi says. If Akin looks at Zunar he'll snort.

"They said we should move to higher ground as soon as possible," Aapa says. "Take any vacant houses we can find. The owners won't be coming back."

Akin laughs and groans at once. All that sneaking around, his gut in his throat for months, mentally practicing what Mother taught him to do if they were ever arrested.

Mother lifts her eyebrows at him and says, "Plans change."

"Some people are out already looking for places," Aaka Katsi says.

Mother stands. "Then Akin and I better get back, before they take ours." She tells them what she and Akin have been doing.

Zunar claps him on the back, and says, "Brilliant!" To Zunar, everything is either "brilliant" or "dismal."

Aaka and Aapa look stricken. Ada snaps her fingernails.

"You've been stealing?" Aaka Katsi whispers.

"They've stolen our labour for years," Mother says, "and, besides, it doesn't matter now."

"Since when is this family a community of two?" Aapa says.

"You would have stood in my way."

Aapa rubs his eyelids. "Sit down, Sela. Please. When you came in we were discussing what to do. Asalie and Narberi want to walk to the university and apply for evacuation."

"Me, too," Tandrea says through her nose.

Akin's aunt Asalie, her mate, Narberi, and their wispy-haired ten-year-old daughter Tandrea live with them. Asalie keeps the child inside, frequently checking her for fever and rash, although Akin can't remember her ever being sick. The incessant step-slap of Tandrea's skipping rope in the common room keeps Akin outdoors as much as possible.

Mother drops back down to her cushion, in her eyes the scoffing look that makes Akin's shoulders tight. "Have the rules changed? We no longer need sponsors on the mainland or immigration approval from another republic?"

"Narberi thinks they'll take pity on a young family," Asalie says. Her clipped and feathery hair reminds Akin of an owl in one of Mother's books.

Akin and Zunar hiked to the university after CONAV took it over to see the new fences all around and the guards at the gate. "An island of indifference," Mother calls it. The only people allowed in are those who qualify for evacuation.

"We'll tell them we're willing to do any job," Narberi says.

"Why would you want to be slaves again?" Mother says.

"We might go, too," Zunar's father, Einar, says. "We need more to eat." His small, pleading eyes look at everyone and no one at once. "You can't count on the right amount of sun and rain. The crops might fail one year, and then what?" Einar is boyish looking from a distance, but close up the strain in his eyes gives his age away. His wife, Tabia, lost so much weight after the government food stores closed, her face is almost cadaverous.

"What if the island sinks completely?" Tandrea says.

Mother turns to her and says with forced patience, "If we don't take a chance on ourselves, others will keep deciding what we're worthy of."

"Sela," Ada says, "would it hurt to at least try? If we can't leave the island, maybe they'll let us live in the dormitories."

"The university gardens are huge," Narberi says, "and CONAV has generators. We'd have food, water, power." He always speaks with authority. Akin envies that, but Mother says not to believe half of what Narberi says. She worked with him at the cannery until it closed.

"The only hospital is there," Asalie says. "What if Tandrea gets sick?"

"We've lost the skills to survive on our own," Katsi says.

"I haven't," Mother says.

"You're free to stay here, Sela," Aapa says, "but Zumi's boy should go with us."

"Akin is free to choose, too," Mother says, but he knows he's not.

His stomach is so tight he can hardly breathe. He can't imagine a life without them all. Before he can say what he wants, which is for everyone to go or everyone to remain, Ada says, "If Sela's staying, so am I." After that, it can only seem he's chosen her over the others.

Mother stands again. "Akin, Ada, and I will secure a house tonight. We'll do our best to hold onto a few others in case you come back." Her mouth hints at a smile as she says, "No applications to file, no criteria to meet for *my* nation."

"Snow Nation," Zunar says, pumping his fist into the air. "It'll be brilliant! I want to go with Akin."

Einar and Tabia look at each other for a long moment, speaking a silent language. "Right, okay," Einar says. "Better to get a house while we can. We can always go to the university tomorrow or the next day."

The others reluctantly agree. Mother has pulled it off.

Later, Asalie complains about not getting the only furnished home. "Take whatever you want from it," Mother says.

Not the chair, not the chair, Akin silently transmits.

That night, as Ada organizes the kitchen – "so good to be out of close quarters, away from all that squabbling," she says – and Mother looks through book after book in the old lady's house, Akin sleeps on the blue recliner by the fireplace. He dreams of The Land. It looks different than it did in the vision. Greener, with lofty trees and cloud-fringed mountains. There are boats, too, coming toward him. Canoes. Where is he, then, that he can greet them?

Only Asalie, Narberi, and Tandrea trek off to the university. They're turned away after waiting with Rainbows from coastal towns up island. The line snaked for half a kilometre, they say. That there were Rainbows without connections gave them comfort, at first: the Snows wouldn't be the only ones left behind. But CONAV has decided to evacuate anyone with a passport and the Rainbows have passports. For days, whenever Akin sees Asalie, her eyes are bright with tears. Why, when the Snows were never encouraged to think they might be able to leave? Why didn't everyone know what Mother did all along?

By September, when three blasts of a haunting horn signal the last ship off the island, most Snows have vacated the Village, caravanning down the catwalks and through the deserted streets with mattresses balanced on their heads and clothing tied around their waists. Mother assumes control of the street she and Akin claimed and someone dubs it Selaville. She won't let more than four or five people move into a house. That's all each garden can support, she says, and, then, only if they strictly ration food and continue to work communal plots.

Aapa and Aaka Katsi have to be satisfied with living next door to Akin in the same house as Asalie's family. On their second night, Aapa and Akin try out the wooden deck behind Aapa's house and the Rainbow custom of sitting in back gardens, hiding from neighbours. They listen to new sounds, to the absence of the slap and drag of the surf. Whenever he hears Aapa's stories about growing up, Akin feels he lived them, too: how puzzling the northern lights seemed when Aapa was a boy in that frozen land; how baffled he was at the wolf's wail and the wind's scream before he knew what they were. For Aapa, as for Akin, mystery and fear sleep in the same bed.

They sit on the wooden slats, hugging their knees, and gaze up at the sky, smeary with stars, more than Akin can ever recall.

"See the Big Dipper?" Akin says.

Aapa follows Akin's finger. "Who told you it was called that?"

"Everybody. At school, everywhere. That's what it is."

"Then everybody is wrong. It's a skin boat, a whaling ship. Those three stars are the boat's deck and the four stars climbing out of it the post you wrap your rope around, the rope attached to your harpoon."

"You ever harpoon a whale?"

"Wasn't old enough, never got a chance before the Great Migration. But, from the time I was ten, I practised shooting harpoons at traps. Each spring I watched the men get ready for the hunt and imagined myself one of them — going off on my own to a private place to sing and pray. They did that, you know, for as long as it took for the ocean to turn whale-calm."

"What did they sing?"

"No one knew. The songs and prayers were secret. Each man made up his own. I got to see them bathe, though. They made themselves so clean they could walk through the village without a dog catching their scent. Every day they'd stand naked in the icy water and scrub their skin with mussels and barnacles. Rubbing off the old to get ready for the new. Some men rubbed their skin raw."

"Weren't they embarrassed, all naked?"

"Nah, only men and boys saw them. And they were showing kinship with the whale. Whales don't wear clothes, you know."

Akin's laugh echoes in the quiet black air.

"We believed the whale would present itself to us so we might continue to live, but only if we showed respect for it and its home. We believed many things once that we seem to have forgotten."

"There's a reason we don't believe everything they did then," Mother says the next day as Akin turns the soil for her medicinal herb garden. "Know what a woman did when her man was on the whale hunt? Stayed in one room like a hostage, forbidden to go out until it was time to cut up the whale meat. Wasn't bad luck for her to do *that*, of course."

Some Snows are at a loss to manage. They were more interested in getting into the once-rich parts of the city – into houses with bidets and long silenced fountains – than in choosing neighbours with survival skills. Aapa visits as many as he can to show them how to care for their rain-water tanks and warn them they should filter and boil the water before drinking. Despite his guidance, nine people on one street take ill with vomiting and diarrhea. Those who care for them get sick, too. Within days, fourteen are dead. It isn't Snow custom to bury their dead in the ground, but no one dares prepare the bodies for ocean committal, so the dead people's neighbours decide to burn them.

On a windy, November afternoon, a few men dig a pit, pile up tires from abandoned cars and lumber stripped from vacant houses. They shovel the bodies and bedding into the pit. Akin and Zunar stand with slack faces as Mother lights a branch and circles the pit with it before touching it to the kindling. "We are the first Snows in a new land," she says. "Death will be our guide."

"Now there's a motto," Zunar whispers to Akin.

Others tend the fire, turning the bodies with shovels and poking them with a pole to make the burning easier. Before long, the skulls explode with a loud noise. That and the smell of burning rubber and flesh make Akin vomit. He isn't the only one. It takes hours for the bodies to turn to ash, leaving only a few pieces of white skull.

Some don't want to live on that street anymore and accuse Mother of having taken the "good" houses. They say she's greedy for disaster, callous for accepting the loss as inevitable and even necessary.

Zunar carves *Death Will Be Our Guide* into a board and nails it above his front door. His parents take it down.

A sense of desolation overwhelms Akin. Everybody is hungry

and uneasy, waiting for something, if only the end of waiting. For the first time, he thinks he might die before his life has meaning.

He dreams of the canoes again. Dreams he sits in one, behind a young woman who turns and smiles at him. He hasn't seen her before but he recognizes her, all the same, from a place deep inside him. Her face is narrow at the forehead, wide at the centre, and her dark eyes slant upward. She has wide, frank lips. "Does freedom mean only death?" he asks, but she doesn't answer.

46 AGM. Akin is alone under the wide, night sky, the only sound the wind – always the wind – as he makes his rounds of Selaville. He circles each house, peering for thieves between rows of parched corn. He and Zunar take turns on guard. They've given each other code-names: Zunar is Fire, and Akin, Water.

His skin gulps down the cool air after the day's heat. Two months of drought, not a cloud to obscure the stars that flicker like the tiny candles Mother leaves in the window when he's on night shift. He tries not to walk a straight path. Randomness is the key, Mother says. Don't be predictable. He and Fire have "brilliant" night vision, can spot a figure, silent as a shadow, creeping in for a beet or a potato.

"If they take it, it's because they need it," Aapa says. He doesn't approve of policing the gardens, of neighbourhoods hoarding water, food, and firewood.

But it's too difficult to share with everyone without rules in place. Easier to stick to your own neighbourhood and work things out there. The work is relentless and tedious. Once you get a good crop going and apportion the water to last through the summer drought, you want to guard what you have. Not all are as good at growing crops as Mother. They don't mix their fire ash into the soil or compost their piss and shit, even though Mother went from house to house at first, teaching the ones who were interested. Some don't know how to make their water last, either. Selaville is the best place to be, for sure, if you don't mind shaving your head. Mother insists on it so there will be one less haven for lice. Fire says it makes them look tough, like guys you shouldn't mess with. Guys with newly deepened voices and carrot breath.

A scraping noise stiffens his spine. Wild dogs are rumoured to run in packs up island. Fear of them keeps the Snows from venturing out of the city. What keeps the dogs from venturing in? But the noise is human, not dog, from a murky shape leaning over the water tank on a roof across the street.

"Hey," he says, sprinting toward the house. He doesn't see the one stepping out of the shadows, doesn't see the knife until it slices the side of his face. It takes a moment for the searing pain to register. He puts his hand up to where it burns and pulls it away covered with blood that looks black in the dark. Yanks off his shirt and presses it to the wound. The intruders are getting away but he's too clammy and dizzy to pursue them. He stumbles a few steps and passes out.

"Was the knife clean?" The first words he hears when he comes to, sticky with sweat. Mother, bathing his wound with warm water that stings and comforts at the same time. He's on a mattress on a floor, a fat white candle in a brass holder to his right. The flame fades in and out, making him nauseous. He closes his eyes.

"I didn't get to inspect it," he says.

"Ha!" Mother said. "You'll be all right."

"Thank mercy," Ada says. He opens his eyes to her frothy hair drifting in and out of focus in the wobbly light thrown by the candle. "Don't put any goop on it until I've stitched it," she whispers.

"He knew what he was doing," Akin says, "the guy with the knife."

"Shh," Ada says as something sharp pierces his skin. His body jerks and he yells.

Mother takes his hands. "Be brave, little boy."

The feel of the thread passing through his flesh is as hard to bear as the needle but Ada is the one who weeps. "That beautiful face," she says.

"Ah, it'll give it some character," Mother says. She kisses his forehead. "I'm proud of you." He's never fallen and cracked his head open like some children, never stepped on a nail in his bare feet, never given her that until now.

She stays with him until morning light, holding his hand and talking, her words rocking him into a kind of surrender. The wound's slightly sweet and rotten smell lurks beneath the scent of lavender salve. Her voice becomes that of the woman in the canoe. Chloe, of the Mountain People. She hated being tall as a child – no, that's Mother – hated being so white, tried to dye her hair black once but it came out purple. Chloe's hair is black. White is a sacred colour, Chloe says. It represents the direction we pass through to the spirit world, a completed cycle. Having children changes you, Mother says. You forget what you once dreamed of being. We invite you to travel to our land and live with us as equals, Chloe says. I'm out of exile at last, Mother says, and Akin feels lighter. He's not all she has, then.

His face heals into a jagged raised scar that throbs when it rains and makes some turn their heads away. "Because you're thieving handsome, now," Fire says. "All the girls want you to poke them."

Akin isn't interested in girls. Dreams of Chloe fill his nights and thoughts of her consume his days. At times he lives in two worlds at once, hearing one voice over his left shoulder, another over his right.

He begins slipping away afternoons, walking the kilometre or two to the edge of the watery lowlands where the sunken city begins. He stares at the deeper, heaving ocean in the distance, searching for the speck that will be Chloe's canoe cresting a wave. He sees only the occasional ship from otherwise invisible CONAV, unconcerned with the Snows as long as they stay clear of the base. Zunar comes with him, at first, but staring bores him. As fall dissolves into winter and the surf smacks against the roofs of swamped buildings, Akin goes alone with an urgency to prepare for whatever is to come. Not what Mother groomed him for from the time he was five: the need to fight side by side with her for Snow rights vanished when they won the city by default. Chloe needs him now.

Mussels anchor their crow-black shells to moss-slicked sidewalks at the edge of flooded areas. Akin pulls a few from their bed, pries them open with a knife and scrapes out the meat, exposing the shell's pearly inside. Thank you, he whispers to the mussels. He removes his shoes and shirt, rolls up his pants to the knee, and wades into the tidal pool. Crouching, he splashes water onto his arms and scrapes his skin until flakes drop into the water. Day by day he removes more clothes until he can stand naked in the water and not shiver. All his senses are heightened, the feel of the air he inhales almost overwhelming. Day by day more cells flake off, exposing new and clean pink skin. He won't stink when she arrives. He'll be pure and respectful. No wild dog will catch his scent.

"The salt water is drying your skin," Mother says.

"Mercy knows what poisons are in there," Ada says.

Stay out of that water, they both say, as though he's an ignorant child. The word *No* rises from his gut into his throat but he's unable to set it free.

The rain flings itself in gusts against windows and roofs that winter, and food stores are insufficient to get anyone beyond hunger. So many suicides make it hard for even Mother to take solace in there being fewer people to feed. Sometimes at night, Akin catches the loose skin on his arm with his teeth and sucks on it. Thievery of winter crops is high, but Water and Fire don't have the heart to stop anyone from yanking a parsnip out of the ground. Snow Nation is fractured, little pieces of despair among ashes of confusion and fatigue. Chloe takes him to The Land where he lies on a soft mattress of earthy smelling fern leaves, listening to the distant sound of drumming. If, as Aapa says, prayers are visits to a peaceful, still place, his dreams are prayers.

In early spring, Akin catches the flu that spreads like a blaze among mostly the young. His body shakes with fever, his dreams a cacophonous torment until Mother – or is it Chloe? – curls up beside him, pressing cool fingers on his forehead and behind his ears, humming in a soft, low voice.

"The wild dogs have stolen your children," Chloe says. "You can steal them back with music." Her words don't make sense. The only missing children have been taken by starvation and disease. Is she scolding him for stopping his ritual cleansing? As soon as he's well, he seeks out his grandfather.

"Dreams are like curtains drawn against a too-bright sun," Aapa says. "You have to look behind them for the meaning. If my mother, your great aaka, Pilipaza, were still alive, she would help you look behind yours."

"When the whalers sang their secret songs, did they play instruments?"

"Yes," Aapa says, surprise lifting his voice. "I'd almost forgotten. Although I never heard them play, they took water drums with them and flutes, rattles. We all sang, you know, not just the whalers."

"She'll want to hear our songs and see our dances," Akin says, "and we don't have any."

Aapa fills an empty can with water and covers it with a piece of a boot. He and Akin carry it down to the water's edge, take turns beating it with their hands and letting out whatever sounds want to escape from their throats: *ah-oh-oh-oh, ay-ay-ay-ay, ah-oh-oh-oh, ay-ay-ay-ay.* Aapa says the sounds have remembered themselves after so many years.

Aaka Katsi and Aapa both come the next day, carrying metal spoons to beat together in time with Akin's drumming. "The visitors will bring smoked fish," Akin tells them. "They will expect us to hold a feast."

Aaka Katsi studies him with her tired, patient eyes and smiles. "Will they, now? My mother used to smoke fish. A few elders might remember how. But when was the last time anyone here caught a fish?"

Aapa leaves and comes back with Einar, Narberi, and a canoe. "These young men have never been fishing," Aapa says, "and I've been too lazy to teach them before. Narberi says he knows where we should look."

Asalie brings Tandrea to see Akin who has begun dancing while he sings and drums. He dances like the seagulls that gather around him, strutting and moving their heads stiffly from side to side. He mimics the eerie shrieks they make when they circle the air, cries of pain and warning. Tandrea spins in one spot, whirling with her arms in the air until she gets dizzy and falls down.

More and more people show up each day with homemade drums and rattles. They try their own tentative dances, stomping their feet and twisting their dwindled bodies, self-conscious at first. Their voices are pocked with suffering. The songs they send up into the clouds sound like cries to the dead. They ask Akin why the Mountain People would choose the Snows to visit. He most wants Mother to hear the answer, but she won't come down to the water.

"Some say the fever took your mind away," she says one morning as he slowly pours water onto a porous, old cloth she holds over a large pot. The cloth is folded into eight layers.

"Too thick," Akin says, his arm aching from the water jug's weight. It takes forever to filter the water and they have to do it every day.

"Just thick enough for the lesson in patience I need," she says. "I've decided to give you some of my rations. Hunger can cause delusions."

Her hands are so bony they could be claws. "Then everyone must be deluded."

She looks up at him with such exhaustion in her eyes he wants the Mountain People to come now, to take Mother back with them and let her rest.

"These people," she says. "When will they arrive?"

"Soon."

"And if they don't?"

"Then, they will come later."

"How can you believe in people you've never seen?"

He shuts his eyes briefly against a sudden sting – she thinks he's crazy, too – and says with more bravado than he feels, "I've never seen the wind, but I know it exists." He cannot wait for her.

The next day he reveals what Chloe told him to those who come to the water's edge. Recites it, afraid to put it in his own words and get it wrong: "The Mountain People seek the one who will fulfill a prophecy. When the White Wolverine Woman's spirit comes to stand upon the earth, they will find the brothers and sisters from whom they were separated thousands of years ago. It will come to pass at the birth of a white wolverine."

No one says Akin's mind is missing. They want to know what a wolverine looks like. Akin doesn't know. Some guess wolf. Narberi is sure it lives up island even though he's never been there. Akin visits each neighbourhood, seeking out those tending gardens and feeder fires and those too weak to work. He tells them of the prophecy and asks if they can describe a wolverine. No one can. He invites them to bring songs and dances to the edge of the sunken city. So many show up, it gets too crowded, so some begin gathering on their own streets. Then several neighbourhoods get together to sing, dance, and share food. People begin sitting in hoops again, talking about what this prophetic wolverine might look like and where they might find it. Many shave their heads in hopes it will show the Mountain People how worthy they are.

Mother complains about Akin taking time away from his chores and about his luring others away from theirs. "What will we live on if you're all off following some dream?"

"Don't you want to sing and dance sometimes, too?" he says.

She turns her head away, wipes her eyes.

"Children can break your heart," Ada says later. "Believe me, I know. Since the time she was your age, she has thought of nothing but those people. Some of them wouldn't be alive if not for her but do they thank her? No. They praise her son, 'the one called Water,' they say. What's wrong with the name she gave you?"

"I'm not that boy anymore."

"You might as well burn her books."

A delegation of elders arrive at the water to say they've determined that an ancestor's spirit has entered Akin's body. They are setting up a schedule of Watchers to post in multiple spots throughout each day to ensure the Snows don't miss the Mountain People's arrival. More food will be needed and, as it is rumoured that orchards of apples, pears, and cherries are not more than a few day's walk away, a few people will arm themselves against the wild dogs and head out in search of the fruit and whatever else they can find. Others will take the few canoes and kayaks they have and head up the coast to look for a white wolverine.

Akin is alone at the water late one afternoon, alone with his doubts and the setting sun, when Mother appears, carrying a book. "Remember this?" she says.

He does. It was as big as his lap when she read it to him, teaching him names of animals he would never see. *Kangaroo, can you say kangaroo?*

Her finger marks a page she opens up to him. "Not a white one," she says, "but it might help those who go searching."

A picture he can't recall. Maybe she thought it would frighten him when he was little. A hairy creature, part bear, part dog, its head too small for its fat body. Deep brown fur with pale yellow streaks along each flank. A disappointing herald.

"It'll be hard to find," she says. "They like isolated places away from humans."

"Fire is trying to talk his father into going on the search with him."

"Aapa thinks the Mountain People are shadows of our deepest desires," she says, closing the book. She holds it out to him with both hands as if in offering.

"What do *you* think?" He takes the book without dropping his gaze from her eyes.

"I think they'll be tired after their journey and need places to stay, food, water."

"Fire asked if I'm the One. I told him I think it's you. The one who kept so many of us from starving."

"There are different kinds of hunger," she says.

"When the Mountain People go back, I'm going with them," he says more defiantly than he intends, but part of him wants to hurt her.

She reaches over and gently traces his scar with her finger. "Your eyes are the very colour I pictured when my Aaka Elin described the morning light on her icy home."

He studies her face as if he were crossing the great water today, never to find his reflection in her again. "Come *with* me," he says. He can see her in The New Land, her long strides carrying her across fields of red, yellow, and blue flowers she's only seen in books, flowers allowed to grow for their beauty alone.

She just smiles. "May I tell you a story?"

He nods warily – she hasn't told him stories for years, but he wants her to stay. He sits cross-legged on the ground. She does the same, facing him, close enough so their knees touch.

"Once upon a time," she says, "a woman gave birth to a child such as her heart had never seen. He was the length of her arm from elbow to wrist and full of infant sweetness."

"Is this a poem?"

"It could be. The child grew into a man such as the world had never seen. He's no longer yours, the world said to her. Be sad, if you must, but proud, and she was."

He closes his eyes and takes in the sounds of life carrying on: birdsong, wind breath, ocean throb. He rises and dances for her then, a new dance: sea spray erupting in joyous spumes.

Backstage

☙❧

An excellent University of Toronto production of *Othello* sparked this collection. I had studied the play years before without having seen it performed. Watching and reflecting on how willingly Desdemona allowed her life to end, I thought of domestic abuse victims and the seeming collusion of some in their own misfortune. Many, like Desdemona, are socially isolated. The story that resulted from that evening – *Nobody; I Myself* – ended up being as much about idealism and racism in the United States in the 1960s as it was about social isolation, but that's the thing about stories: they often end up being about something other than what you intended.

So it was with *Not Meant to Know*. Miranda in *The Tempest* isn't a particularly complex character. She exists dramatically to become Ferdinand's bride and thus help his father and hers reconcile. She falls in love with the first good-looking guy she meets. Boring. What interested me, initially, was how she would relate to that guy, not having had any female role models in her life from the age of three. I intended to tell the story of a girl who is kept hidden from the world by her father but, as I began to write, it morphed into something else.

Other stories were triggered by questions I had about specific characters. For example, what was behind Gertrude's hasty marriage to her husband's brother in *Hamlet*? She doesn't come across well in the play, primarily because we see her through Hamlet's eyes. She has overstepped gender bounds by not remaining grief-stricken and devoted to her husband's memory. We don't see her inner conflict. Her son's struggle is the heart of the play. It's possible her second marriage was a pragmatic move. Denmark is under threat of invasion by the prince of Norway. It wasn't as if Hamlet could take the red eye from Wittenberg to assume the throne and defend the kingdom. In *Passing Through*, I give my Gertrude a chance to explain herself, time to reflect on what's important to her.

In *Silent Girl*, the question sprang from the improbable plot of *Pericles*. The hero's wife, presumed dead, is buried at sea yet turns up later, alive and untouched by another man, having hidden herself in a temple to the goddess Diana. His daughter, Marina, is kidnapped by pirates and sold to a brothel yet retains her virginity. Shakespeare didn't shirk from revealing incest between King Antiochus and his daughter. Why, then, leave Marina's virtue intact? This was the incongruity that fuelled *Silent Girl*. Researching the story was painful, writing it even more so. I am stunned by the scope and range of the sex slave trade that isn't happening only "over there, somewhere." In North America, tens of thousands of women and girls are kidnapped or coerced into sexual slavery every year.

Kidnapping also figures in *Kesh Kumay*. I had been searching for a modern counterpart to *The Taming of the Shrew's* Kate whose abdication to Petruchio at the end of the play always makes me squirm in empathetic humiliation. By lucky accident I caught Petr Lom's illuminating and moving documentary *The Kidnapped Brides* on CBC's *Passionate Eye*. When one woman tells Lom, "After the kidnapping, you've no choice – you start loving, even if you don't want to, you have to build a life," I knew I had found my Kate in post-Soviet Kyrgyzstan.

The Winter's Tale, like *Shrew*, presents a problem for feminist sensibilities. Hermione's husband Leontes falsely accuses her of adultery and locks her up in prison where she gives birth to their second child, a daughter. He orders the baby taken out into the wilds and left for animals to feed upon. When he gets word Hermione is dead and their first child has died of a broken heart over separation from his mother, he repents and goes into protracted grieving. Too darn late, you think, forgetting this is a romance. In the last act – which takes place sixteen years later – we learn Hermione is alive and has been in hiding. She reveals herself to Leontes as a statue that comes to life and they stroll off into happily-ever-after land, she apparently having forgiven all of his treachery. Pondering Hermione's sixteen years of fealty to an unhealthy relationship led me to imagine, in *Deep Dark Waves,* another woman's suspended animation. Through research I learned of a tendency in social work circles to deny that some women are violence-prone, resulting in a scarcity of therapeutic services to help them and their families.

I was intrigued with the atypical mothering of Volumnia in *Coriolanus.* Thinking I would work with some of feminist bell hook's theories about the continued disempowerment of North American blacks, I envisioned a story about gang culture. That it evolved into *The Snow People*, a parable about oppression in an environmentally degraded future, I can only attribute to alchemy.

Cocktails with Charles allowed me to explore the complexities and fluid boundaries of gender. *Twelfth Night* is one of Shakespeare's "trouser plays," as a writer friend calls them: plays in which women disguise themselves as men either to be able to travel without molestation or to gain entry into the privileged world of men. It's laughable that they get away with it, but the plays are comedies, after all. In my comedy I wanted my characters to get away with breaking old patterns to find new meaning.

It became apparent to me as I got deeper into the research and writing of this collection that some things haven't changed for women since Shakespeare's time. The reason, I suspect, is that we are still locked into gender roles and a patriarchal value system despite the efforts of many women and men to change their thinking and their behaviour. We need different kinds of stories – a new mythology, perhaps – to free us.

Glossary of Terms

⊰⊱

NOT MEANT TO KNOW

Junket—brand name of a rennet-based pudding.
White Castle—self-declared first hamburger fast-food chain, offering hamburgers for five cents each in 1921.

SILENT GIRL

Anh—a Cajun reply when one does not understand, or an expression of surprise.
Chirren—Cajun for children.
Dipped in de Bayou—Cajun for unsophisticated.
Duckanary—a made-up word.
Empress of Heaven, Goddess of the Sea, Ma-tsu—the patron saint of seafarers in Taiwan; she began as a real person born in 960 who, because she didn't cry until more than a month old, was named Lin Muo (*muo* meaning silence) and often referred to as Muo-niang ("the silent girl"). According to legend, when she was sixteen years old she received some kind of initiation from Heaven and was given a bronze amulet. After that she could ward off evil spirits, forestall calamities, heal the weak and the sick, and save imperilled fishing boats. It's said that if you call one of her names, she will appear to help you. If you call her as Empress

of Heaven, she will be delayed coming to your aid by having to dress in her finery.

Guff—Cajun for the Gulf of Mexico.

Le souper—Cajun for supper.

Peeshwank—Cajun for runt.

Poodoo—Cajun for no class.

Make do-do—Cajun for go to sleep.

Ohm—Cajun for home.

Phi Phi Don—an island in Thailand between Phuket and the Andaman Sea coast of the mainland.

T—Cajun for little when affixed to first name.

KESH KUMAY

Ayee—exclamation of excitement.

Ala Kachuu—bride kidnapping, a common practice in rural Kyrgyzstan in the struggling post-Soviet economy as it reduces wedding costs. Some brides are willing participants (as they are in western elopements). For those who are not, the practice is illegal, but the police seem reluctant to enforce the law.

Ama—affectionate name for mother.

Ata—affectionate name for father.

Bishkek—a wooden stick used to churn mare's milk as it ferments into *koumiss*; also the name of Kyrgyzstan's capital city which was renamed after the wooden stick in 1991. Between 1926 and 1991 the capital was known as Frunze in honour of a Bolshevik military leader.

Chai—milky, spiced tea.

Chanach—pouch made of animal skins that have been cleaned and smoked over a fire of pine branches to give *koumiss* a special smell and taste.

Erf—exclamation of disgust.

Jailoo—mountain pasture, 2500 meters or more above sea level, used by Kyrgyz nomads in summer to graze flocks of sheep, horses and cows.

Jooluk—ceremonial white scarf tied around a kidnapped bride's head to indicate her acceptance of the marriage.

Kalpak—hat made from four panels of white felt with traditional patterns stitched into it as decoration. It is worn by males of all ages, especially in rural Kyrgyzstan, and is a symbol of the nation's history. Plain white ones are often reserved for festivals and special occasions. Others intended for everyday use may have a black lining.

Kesh Kumay—"kiss the girl" or "chasing the kiss"—a traditional folk game in which a man on horseback tries to catch a woman on horseback and kiss her.

Komuz—an ancient fretless string instrument used in Kyrgyz music, closely related to other Turkic string instruments and the lute.

Koumiss—the traditional drink of Kyrgyzstan, made from fermenting milk in a *chanach*. It is mildly alcoholic.

Manas—the hero of one of the world's great pieces of oral literature, *The Epic of Manas*, twenty times longer than *The Odyssey*. For centuries it was recited. The first full written version appeared only in the 1920s. In the '30s through the '50s, *The Manas* was eliminated from school curricula and certain parts of it were re-interpreted to support communist philosophy. Manas was a Khan of the Kyrgyz, reputedly born in the Talas region of northern Kyrgyzstan. The story relates his trying to create a homeland for his people and fighting off various neighbouring hordes.

Manaschi—professional and highly valued reciters of *The Epic of Manas*.

Oomiyen—amen.

Shirdak—traditional felt rug made by sewing patterns of contrasting felt together using patterns often inspired from nature such as mountains, animal horns, and birds. Shirdaks are used by the nomadic Kyrgyz to decorate yurts.

Som—the currency of the Republic of Kyrgyzstan. The som was introduced in 1993, replacing the Russian ruble. The word means "pure" in Kyrgyz and implies pure gold.

Ulak Tartysh—wrestling on horseback for the carcass of a sheep or goat. Two teams of an equal number of riders play on a field that is 300 meters long and 150 meters wide. The opposite sides of this area are the "gates," marked with flags. Placed in the center of the field is a carcass of a goat or sheep, weighing an average of 30-40 kilograms. One game is 15 minutes long. The objective is to seize the animal carcass and deliver it into the gates of the contesting team. The players are allowed to pick up the carcass from any place within the limits of the field, take it from their rivals, pass it or fling it over to their partners, carry it pressed to the horse's side or suspended between the horse's legs.

Yurt—traditional felt tent-like home of nomads who live on the steppes of Central Asia. Wooden poles connect the latticework walls on the bottom of the yurt to the hole in the middle of the tent for the smoke to escape and light to enter. The wood frame is then covered with felt and sometimes with canvas.

DEEP DARK WAVES

Hickety, Pickety, My Black Hen—an English nursery rhyme and child's song: *Hickety pickety, my black hen / She lays eggs for gentlemen; / Sometimes nine, sometimes ten, / Hickety pickety, my black hen.*

NOBODY; I MYSELF

AME **church**—African Methodist Episcopal Church founded in Philadelphia in 1816.
Conked hair—hair straightened with chemicals.

COCKTAILS WITH CHARLES

Mentsch—Yiddish for decent human being.
Meshuge—Yiddish for crazy, senseless.
Tukhes—Yiddish for buttocks.

THE SNOW PEOPLE: 30-46 AGM

Aaka—grandmother.

Aapa—grandfather.

Air scooter—based on the Air Scooter II lightweight helicopter available now through a company in Nevada.

CONAV—short for the naval forces of the fictitious coalition of Pacific Republics.

Digital guardian—based on current identification, location tracking, and condition monitoring technology.

Dimethyl Sulphide—a biological sulphur compound emitted over the ocean by phytoplankton.

Electric shields—based on shields in current use for riot control.

Holovision—based on 3D technology under development now.

Mid-Norte—a fictitious republic encompassing the former central region of the USA.

New Columbia—a fictitious republic encompassing the former province of British Columbia and the states of Washington and Oregon.

Prairie Shield—a fictitious republic encompassing the former provinces of Alberta and Saskatchewan.

Refugia—locations of remnant populations of once widespread animal or plant species.

Skin boat—type of boat dating back thousands of years; modern ones are made of wood and nylon or other cloth instead of animal skins.

Sky car—based on Moller International's M400 Skycar, a personal vertical takeoff and landing vehicle.

Tayberry—cross between a blackberry and a raspberry.

Note: Readers can find discussion guides for each of the stories at www.triciadower.com.

Acknowledgements

CRBED

MANY THANKS TO:

My husband Colin Dower who, with love, philosophy, and plenty of snacks, saw me through the three years it took to complete this collection.

Fellow writer Larry Connolly who, as the first professional reader of each story, made sure I did not go outside with my slip showing, so to speak. His humour, candour, and insight have been invaluable.

The talented and supportive members of my writing group in Victoria: Leanne Baugh-Peterson, Susan Braley, Diana Jones, and Marybeth Nelson who laboured with me through sometimes multiple versions of these stories and have joyously journeyed with me each step of the publication process.

Early readers of multiple stories: Martin Cloutier, Susan DiPlacido, T. J. Forrester, Steven Gajadhar, Steve Hughes, Liesl Jobson, Barbara Milton, Tripp Reade, Brandi Reissenweber, Brian Reynolds, Danna Layton Sides, Diane Smith, and Andrew Tibbetts – most, fellow participants in the Zoetrope Virtual Studio for which I thank its sponsor, Francis Ford Coppola.

My son Mike Wolfgang, daughter Katie Wolfgang, daughter-in-law Kate O'Rourke, son-in-law Carman Lawrick, sister and brother-in-law Lillian and Glenn Dobbs, and friends Suzie Labonne,

Nancy Swartz, Don Pinder, and Wayne McNulty for believing in me, even when I didn't. An extra thank you to Katie for lending her professional expertise to the book promotion.

Ashley and CC for saying "cool" when hearing about Grandma's book.

Luciana Ricciutelli, Editor-in-Chief, and the board of directors of Inanna Publications for their enthusiastic acceptance and support of *Silent Girl*.

William Shakespeare, wherever he is.

Photo: Destrubé

Tricia Dower's fiction has appeared in *Room of One's Own, The New Quarterly, Hemispheres, Cicada, NEO, Insolent Rudder,* and *Big Muddy.* Having explored various North American locations, she now lives and writes in Victoria, British Columbia. *Silent Girl* is her first book.